PRESENTED IN LOVING
MEMORY OF
HUNTER E. DOYLE

The
ISLAND
at the END of
EVERYTHING

ALSO BY KIRAN MILLWOOD HARGRAVE

The Girl of Ink & Stars

The
ISLAND
at the END of
EVERYTHING

Kiran Millwood Hargrave

Alfred A. Knopf　New York

THIS IS A BORZOI BOOK PUBLISHED BY ALFRED A. KNOPF

Visit us on the Web! rhcbooks.com

Educators and librarians, for a variety of teaching tools,
visit us at RHTeachersLibrarians.com

Library of Congress Cataloging-in-Publication Data
Names: Hargrave, Kiran Millwood, author.
Title: The island at the end of everything / Kiran Millwood Hargrave.
Description: First American edition. | New York : Alfred A. Knopf, [2018]. |
"Originally published in the United Kingdom by Chicken House Publishing
Ltd. in 2017"—Title page verso. | Summary: When the Philippine government
takes over Culion, an island for people with leprosy, Ami is put in an
orphanage on another island, where she finds a friend willing to help her
return before her mother dies.
Identifiers: LCCN 2017021578 (print) | LCCN 2017037652 (ebook) |
ISBN 978-0-553-53532-7 (trade) | ISBN 978-0-553-53533-4 (lib. bdg.) |
ISBN 978-0-553-53534-1 (ebook)
Subjects: | CYAC: Mothers and daughters—Fiction. | Leprosy—Fiction. |
Friendship—Fiction. | Orphanages—Fiction. | Culion Island (Philippines)—
History—20th century—Fiction. | Philippines—History—20th century—
Fiction. | BISAC: JUVENILE FICTION / Action & Adventure / General.
Classification: LCC PZ7.1.H368 (print) | LCC PZ7.1.H368 Isl 2018 (ebook) |
DDC [Fic]—dc23

The text of this book is set in 10-point Cabrito Didone.

Printed in the United States of America
April 2018
10 9 8 7 6 5 4 3 2 1

First Edition

For my husband

The world shall perish not for lack of
wonders, but for lack of wonder.

J. B. S. Haldane

Glossary

Nanay . . . . Mother

Ama . . . . Father

Lolo . . . . Grandfather

Gumamela . . Hibiscus, a kind of flower common
in the Philippines

Tadhana . . . . Fate

Takipsilim . . . Twilight

Habilin . . . . . . Something given to someone for safekeeping

Lihim . . . . Secret

Diwata . . . . . . Guardian spirits, usually of nature

Pitaya . . . . Dragon fruit

Pahimakas . . . Last farewell

The
ISLAND
at the END of
EVERYTHING

CULION ISLAND,
THE PHILIPPINES
1906

There are some places you would not want to go.

Even if I told you that we have oceans clear and blue as summer skies, filled with sea turtles and dolphins, or forest-covered hills lush with birds that call through air thick with warmth. Even if you knew how beautiful the quiet is here, clean and fresh as a glass bell ringing. But nobody comes here because they want to.

My *nanay* told me this is how they brought her, but says it is always the same, no matter who you are or where you come from.

From your house you travel on horse or by foot, then on a boat. The men who row it cover their noses and mouths with cloths stuffed with herbs so they don't have to share your breath. They will not help you onto the boat although your head aches and two weeks ago your legs began to hurt, then to numb. Maybe you stumble toward them, and they duck. They'd rather you rolled over their backs and into the sea than touch you. You sit and clutch your bundle of things from home, what you saved before it was burned. Clothes, a doll, some books, letters from your mother.

Somehow, it is always dusk when you approach.

The island changes from a dark dot to a green heaven on the horizon. High on a cross-topped cliff that slopes toward the sea is a field of white flowers, looping strangely. It is not until you are closer that you see it forms the shape of an eagle, and it is not until you are very close that you see it is made of stones. This is when your heart hardens in your chest, like petals turning to pebbles. Nanay says the white eagle's meaning is known across all the surrounding islands, even all the places outside our sea. It means: *Stay away. Do not come here unless you have no choice.*

The day is dropping to dark as you come into the harbor. When you step from the boat, the stars are setting out their little lights. Someone will be there to welcome you. They understand.

The men who brought you leave straightaway, though they are tired. They have not spoken to you in the days or hours you spent with them. The splash of oars fades to the sound of waves lapping the beach. They will burn the boat when they get back, as they did your house.

You look at the person who greeted you. You are changed now. Like flowers into stones, day into night. You will always be heavier, darkened, marked. Touched.

Nanay says that in the Places Outside, they have many names for our home. The Island of the Living Dead. The Island of No Return. The Island at the End of Everything.

You are on Culion, where the oceans are blue and clear as summer skies. Culion, where sea turtles dig the beaches and the trees brim with fruit.

Culion, island of lepers. Welcome home.

A Visitor

I am luckier than most. I was born here, so I never had to know the name-calling, the spitting in the street. My *nanay* was already carrying me when they came for her, though she didn't know it until she stepped from the boat a month after leaving home and felt a flutter in her stomach, like wings. Me, growing.

Nanay was one of the first to arrive, was brought even before the eagle. She helped build it when I was small, barely tumbled from her and wrapped tightly onto her back. When they plucked the sun-bleached coral rocks from the shore, they were just stones. Now they are a bird.

I tell Nanay this when she is afraid, which is often, though she tries to hide it. *See*, I tell her, *that bird is all stone the color of bone, and it is beautiful.* What I mean is that even as her body melts away from her, down to its bones, she is still beautiful. Nanay says back, *But that bird's meaning is not so beautiful, is it? It's the symbol of the Department of Health. It means we are a cursed island, an island of illness.*

I wish she sometimes wouldn't make things sad straight-away.

I've noticed that grown-ups often reach for the bad side of things. At school, Sister Clara's lessons are full of sins and devils, not love and kindness like in Sister Margaritte's classes, even though they are both teaching us God and Church. Sister Margaritte is the most important nun on the island, and the kindest, so I choose to listen to her rather than Sister Clara.

Nanay has other gods, small ones she keeps on the window-sill or under her pillow. She does not like me going to church, but the sisters insist. And anyway, I like Sister Margaritte. She has a wide mouth and the cleanest fingernails I've ever seen. *You have a very serious face,* she said once after prayer, but she did not say it in a way that was unkind. Nanay says I squint so much I'll give myself lines, but I can't help that I squint when I think.

My face is scrunching now, but that's because of the sun. I have found a clearing in the trees that edge our yard where I can kneel so my body is cool in the shade and my face can tip up to blue. It is Sunday-day-of-rest, so I don't have school, and church isn't for an hour.

I'm watching for butterflies. Nanay and I have been plant-

8

ing flower seeds on the wild land beside the bakery for three summers, but they still haven't sprouted. Nanay says the soil must be wrong for growing the plants butterflies like. I still have never seen one anywhere in town. I'm certain they're always wafting behind me, just as your shadow disappears when you suddenly spin around. So I'm being still whenever I can remember.

"Amihan!"

"Out here, Nanay."

Nanay looks tired and her skin is stretched around the eyes. She used my full name, and her blue cloth is wrapped across her face, which means we have a visitor. It is a not-nice fact, but her nose is nearly not there anymore. When she breathes, it sounds as if the air has hooks. Being Touched means different things for different people: for some, it's sores like pink ink splotches on their arms and legs; for others, it's bumps like they've fallen into a patch of stinging leaves or angered a wasps' nest. For Nanay, it's her nose and swollen fingers, and pain, though she's good at hiding it.

"Sister Clara is here to see us," she says. "Dust off your knees and come inside."

I brush my trousers down and follow her. The room is hot, and Nanay has placed bowls of water under the windows to cool it. Sister Clara is standing by the open front door and does not come in even when I arrive. Dr. Tomas told everyone that you can't become Touched by inhaling the same air, but I don't think Sister Clara believes him, because she never goes near my *nanay* or any of the others. Then again, she never goes near me, either, though I am Untouched. I think perhaps she doesn't like children, which seems strange for a nun, especially a nun who's a teacher.

"Hello, Sister Clara," I say, as we have been taught to, in a voice that is almost song.

"Amihan," says Sister Clara. It is meant to be a greeting, but it comes out flat.

"Is she in trouble, Sister?" snaps Nanay through her cloth. "What is it this time? Running in school? Laughing in church?"

"There's to be a meeting in church this afternoon. Service will be cut short," replies Sister Clara coolly. "Attendance is compulsory."

"Anything else?"

Sister Clara shakes her head and leaves with a damning "God bless you."

Nanay slams the door shut behind her with her stick. "God bless *you.*"

"Nanay!"

Her forehead is sweating. She unwraps her face cloth, hangs it on the doorknob and collapses into her chair. "I'm sorry, Ami. But that woman—" She stops herself. She wants to say something she shouldn't, and continues carefully, "I don't like her."

"What are you going to wear for the service?" I say, trying to distract her. She gets upset when people treat her like Sister

Clara just did: as if she's something to be skirted around, not looked in the eye.

"Same as last time, I suppose."

Last time was a long time ago, when the nuns first started working here. Half my lifetime. I help Nanay up and she limps into our room to change, muttering. She is so angry I do not dare offer to help her with her buttons.

I change too, into my blue dress. Nanay is wearing her next-best dress, which I suppose is her way of showing what she thinks of church.

"We could take more flower seeds," I say to fill the silence. "Sow the butterfly garden a bit more?"

"I'm not wasting any more time on that. Not a single butterfly came last summer, Ami," says Nanay. "I don't think they like it on Culion."

We sit quietly in our best and next-best clothes, and wait until it is time to go.

The Meeting

Church is the most beautiful building on the island. I like it here because it is always cool inside, even now when the sun is heating the sand to coals on the beach below. The walls shine white like the center of coral. To see it glowing like a beacon at the top of the hill makes the last, steep stretch easier, though Nanay found it harder than her last visit.

We are sitting behind Capuno and Bondoc, who live down the street from us. Nanay has not said "Amen" even once, or stood when she is meant to, though this may be because she is sore from the climb. The other children from school are sitting at the back, all together in one big clump like they do after class. When we came in, the girls bent their heads together and whispered. I know they think I'm strange because I don't stay to play after school, but Nanay needs me to help her at home. I slide my hand into hers and squeeze. She's all the friends I need—though I sometimes wish the girls wouldn't whisper.

Father Fernan is about to start the final part of his sermon. This week it is about temperance, which I think means not drinking alcohol, because it makes God sad when you sing loudly in the street. I hope Bondoc is listening, because though his name means "mountain" and he looks like a mountain, he sings like a strangled goat.

Capuno and Bondoc are brothers. Capuno is Touched, Bondoc is not, but he followed his brother to Culion anyway. Capuno is as small as Bondoc is big, but he has a quiet energy about him, an undertow. They are two of the kindest men I know, even if they do sing in the street through lack of temperance.

"So remember, next time you pass the tavern," Father Fernan intones, "tip your hat to the owner and turn up your palms to God. Let us pray."

I go to bow my head, but Nanay unclasps my fingers and crosses her arms. The sisters do not notice because we are told to look down to talk to God, even though apparently He is above our heads in Heaven.

Father Fernan makes the sign of the cross over us. There is silence for a moment as everyone wonders what is going to come next. Father Fernan rearranges his somber expression into a smile. People sit a little less straight and murmur to each other. Nanay uncrosses her arms slightly. They are marked where her fingernails dug in. Sister Clara sits beside the pulpit while Sister Margaritte sets up another three chairs and then settles in one.

There is the sound of footsteps up the aisle, and a man I have not seen before passes us with Dr. Tomas, whose face is solemn. The stranger is wearing a pale linen suit and carries two wooden planks. He walks like a marionette, picking his feet up high, then sits on one of the chairs, head-string pulled taut. We all look at Father Fernan expectantly.

"Thank you for joining us," he begins, as if we have only just arrived. "We are here to discuss some very important changes that will be taking place in Culion Town. These changes may seem strange at first, but we must remember God's plan, and trust in Him."

Sister Clara nods gravely, but Sister Margaritte's wide mouth is sealed thinly shut as an envelope, and Dr. Tomas looks pained, his face scrunched up like a chewed toffee.

"Sitting beside Dr. Tomas is our special guest, Mr. Zamora." Everyone's heads swivel. "Mr. Zamora works for the government in Manila. He is going to share with you the future of our island."

The stranger unfolds from his chair. He is so long and thin he looks like a locust standing upright. His hands jangle limply from his wrists as he steps forward and takes off his hat, which he shouldn't really have been wearing inside anyway.

"Patients and families," he starts, and I already know this is not going to be a good meeting. Nobody who lives here thinks

14

of the Touched as patients, except maybe Sister Clara. "Thank you for having me. I very much enjoyed the service."

His voice is full and low, at odds with his skinny frame, his lips puffy as a fish's. Nanay is tense again beside me, and in front Bondoc leans back on the hard wooden pew and crosses his arms.

"Father Fernan is right that I am here to tell you about some very important changes, but he neglected to mention that they are also exciting. We, the government, are moving Culion toward a place of en-light-en-ment." He strikes each beat of the word on his palm. "Progress is being made in the fight against the affliction that many of you suffer from. With all due respect to Dr. Tomas, the methods used to treat the disease are evolving very fast outside this colony. We already know that leprosy is caused by a bacterium, and I am sure Dr. Tomas has advised you all that cleanliness is paramount. We are hopeful that within the life span of your children, we will find a cure for lepers."

There is a collective intake of breath and Nanay flinches. We do not use that word. My palms itch. It is suddenly stifling inside the church.

"But until that day, changes must be made. We must prevent the spread of the disease. It has been brought to the government's attention that many of you are breeding. I know that Father Fernan and the sisters will have advised you about the merits of abstinence, but what of those children who are born without the disease? Must they, too, live the life of a leper?"

He has found his rhythm now, striding across the front of the church on his needle-thin legs, hands waving. Meanwhile, we have stopped sitting silently. People are hissing angrily, the noise rising like spit on hot coals. Nanay takes my hand and squeezes.

"We say no!" Mr. Zamora continues, as if the hissing were applause. "We are going to save Culion's innocents and give them a better life. Is that not what all parents want? A better life for their children? From here on, we will facilitate this through a process of segregation."

He swoops suddenly on the wooden planks beside his chair and holds them up, one in each hand. On one is written *SANO*. On the other, *LEPROSO*.

Bondoc stands up, more mountain-like than ever. His body is trembling as he shrugs off Capuno's restraining hand and forces his way into the aisle, striding to within a foot of Mr. Zamora. I think he might hit him, but he just stands, fingers clenched into fists.

"What is the meaning of this?" he says furiously. Sister Margaritte has stood up too and is beside him, speaking soothingly. Mr. Zamora twitches his fish lips into a smile.

"I was just about to explain," he says.

"Well, explain. And choose better words than the ones you have already used," says Bondoc, allowing Sister Margaritte to lead him to a space on the front pew.

"Please, this is our guest—" starts Father Fernan, but Mr. Zamora raises his hand the way Sister Clara does to us in school, and inclines his head in an *of course.* He displays the planks again.

"*Sano*—clean. *Leproso*—leper," he says.

"We can read," mutters Capuno.

"Many of these signs will be placed around the island. Those who are clean must stay in the areas marked *Sano.* Those who are lepers must keep to their designated places."

"But what of the families?" Nanay drops my hand and stands with the suddenness of Bondoc, but she does not approach Mr. Zamora.

"I'm sorry?"

"What of the families?"

"I can't hear you." He can. We all know he can.

Nanay must know that too, but after only a moment's pause she unwraps the cloth around her face. She can be very brave when she needs to be. Sister Clara looks away with a tut, but Mr. Zamora stares in a way that is even worse.

"I said, what about the families? I have *bred.* My *clean* daughter has been living with me, her demonstrably *dirty* mother, for all her life. She has remained *clean,* despite the best attempts of my *affliction* to sully her. What do you propose be done?"

Her voice is a challenge, with the point of a sword on her tongue.

Mr. Zamora wets his lips. "This was what I was going to address next, before your interruption."

Nanay inhales deeply to reply but Father Fernan stands up

and opens his hands, like when he is demonstrating God opening His heart to us.

"Please, child. Let our guest finish."

It is a betrayal. I feel this, as certain as the sweat on my palms. He is betraying us. Nanay sinks back down and does not take my hand again, so I squeeze her wrist to show her I am proud.

"This is all in aid of reducing the spread of *Mycobacterium leprae*," Mr. Zamora says importantly. "The disease that has taken your nose. Is that your daughter beside you?" He does not wait for an answer. "How would you feel if she ended up looking like that?"

Someone has to say something, but my voice is caught in my throat. Sister Margaritte makes an involuntary movement, and Father Fernan holds up his hand to her the way Mr. Zamora did to him as the stranger continues to pace.

"We are doing this not for our pleasure, oh, no. This place is a drain on the government's finances, but we have given you a beautiful home."

"We have been here for years!" calls out Bondoc. "Generations, in some cases. You haven't *given* us anything—"

Mr. Zamora talks over him. "We are introducing the segregation to save the innocents." I do not understand why he keeps using that word. "We will give those who are healthy a future. I have been given control of a facility on Coron Island—"

Coron: our neighboring island. You can sight it on a clear day—and we have many clear days—from the eastern hills.

But it is only a low smudge, as if a greasy finger has been wiped across the faraway glass of the horizon. It is too far to wave from one beach to another and see each other.

"Facility?" interrupts Sister Margaritte. "Like an asylum?"

"An orphanage," says Mr. Zamora.

"But these children, they have parents." The nun's voice is shaking. Nanay grips my hand. "Their parents aren't dead."

"But they are *sick*, Sister. And they live in what will become the largest leper colony in the world within three years, if our projections are correct. I am piloting this scheme on Coron, taking over an orphanage, to give the Culion children a better quality of life. They will live with other healthy children, away from sickness and death. When they grow up, they will be able to have jobs on the mainland, in Manila and further abroad. The disease will die out—"

"You mean *we* will die out, Mr. Zamora?" Capuno's voice is soft, but the challenge halts the man in his tracks. He stares down at Capuno, and his silence is worse than a nod. There is another collective flinch as he continues.

"This segregation has the full weight of the government behind it. Father Fernan has given his blessing and only this morning Dr. Tomas signed an agreement that already has seventy signatures from world experts from America, India, China and Spain."

The priest and the doctor keep their faces turned to the floor as Mr. Zamora pulls an envelope from his breast pocket, brandishing what I assume is the agreement. Dr. Tomas has signed this. Father Fernan has blessed this. Experts from countries far beyond our sea have agreed to it. The whole world is against us.

"They are all of the opinion that this is the best—no, the *only*—course of action. Reinforcements from the government will be arriving to ensure it all goes smoothly. The sisters will bring you, street by street, to the hospital for your assessment. This is the start of a new era."

This is the end. No one is hissing or standing up to question Mr. Zamora. The planks are propped up against the step before the pulpit.

Sano. Leproso.

I have forgotten how to breathe.

Article XV

The next morning bamboo posts have sprung up at the end of every street. A notice written on large wooden boards is nailed to each. At the top are maps of Culion Island, with red circles showing where the *Sano* and *Leproso* areas are. All the boards say the same, over and over. I tore one down and brought it to Nanay, whose foot was giving her too much trouble for her to get out of bed and see them for herself.

ARTICLE XV, CHAPTER 37
OF THE ADMINISTRATIVE CODE
Segregation of Persons with Leprosy

I. All persons on Culion Island must be subjected to medical inspection to determine the presence or absence of leprosy.

II. If it be found that a person has leprosy, they shall be marked for segregation within the *Leproso* areas in Culion Town. Trespassing into *Sano* areas is strictly prohibited.

III. If it be found that an adult (over the age of eighteen years) does not have leprosy, the Director of Health authorizes this person to remain in Culion Town within the *Sano* areas. Limited trespass may be made into *Leproso* areas under authorized supervision.

IV. If it be found that a child (under the age of eighteen years) does not have leprosy, they shall enter the care of the Director of Health or his authorized representative. In this instance, they will be transported to the CORON ORPHANAGE.

There are other rules too, but I stop reading after point IV. This tells me all I need to know because I am under eighteen, and so must go to Coron. At the bottom of each notice is written in red:

BY THE POWER AFFORDED MR. N. ZAMORA BY THE DIRECTOR OF HEALTH, THESE LAWS WILL COME INTO EFFECT AT CULION LEPER COLONY WITHIN TWENTY-EIGHT DAYS.

When she has read it, Nanay gets me to chop it up for firewood, but the words stay branded on my mind. I wonder about the person whose job it was to paint the words on the boards, if they realized that their day's work has rewritten the rest of my life. Or was it like when you get lines in class for talking or being late, and the words turn to spiders beneath your fingers, their meaning scuttling away across the paper?

I thought I had dreamt it all. Sister Clara's visit, the meeting, Mr. Zamora. I woke up the next morning and thought maybe I had been in the sun too long and my head had filled with heat that cooked my brain. But school has been canceled until segregation has been completed, and these boards are real.

Nanay crying in bed is not a dream. Bondoc and Capuno wailing outside our house after a night in the tavern is not a dream. Bondoc will have to move to the *Sano* side of town, away from his home, away from us—or rather from Nanay. Capuno keeps saying he does not understand.

I understand, and I have not cried. I have shrunk inside, all my tears dry and stuck, like a nut lodged in my throat. I wonder about the other children with Touched parents, if they feel the same weight crumpling their chests.

Because Nanay is in her dark place and the walls feel too close inside, I go back to the patch of warm earth at the end of our garden. The trees have dropped small berries in the night. I know not to eat them but they are a beautiful purple, so I collect handfuls in my skirt.

There are thirty, the same years Nanay is. I pair them and race each pair down the slope of the clearing, over and over until I have only three left. They all roll quickly down the slope but eventually I have an overall winner. It is no different from the others in size or color. There are no nicks in its surface, nor is it smoother, but it wins each time. I wonder what makes it different.

I lie on my back and follow the shifting patch of sun with my head until it drops past our house and the light goes flat. I keep the winning berry in my hand the whole time. It grows warm and slick and soon it has been there so long I can't remember where my hand stops and it begins. The trees throw their shadows across the ground, and the clouds are nailed so loosely to the darkening sky they come apart in places. I see a pig's snout in one, and a flying fish with an extra fin that shifts to a boat when I squint.

Then the sky fades and I think more about Mr. Zamora, though I don't want to. I think about Dr. Tomas and Father Fernan sitting in silence, and Sister Margaritte, her wide mouth tight as a fishing line.

When it is night, Nanay calls for me to come inside and I jump. The berry bursts in my palm.

The Test

The next day Sister Margaritte comes to collect Nanay and me for testing. Although Nanay is obviously Touched, she has to be checked by the government's doctors so they can give her identification papers. Sister Margaritte tells us that in the Places Outside—all the other islands that make up our country, which we learn about in school—the Touched are being collected together and sent on ships to Culion.

She embraces Nanay when she opens the door. She looks almost as sad as my mother, her head shrunken in her habit, like a baby in swaddling. I worry Nanay will be rude because she doesn't like the nuns, but she doesn't even tense up. Instead she goes slack in Sister Margaritte's arms. They exchange quiet words in quiet voices that mean I should not listen, so I stay in our bedroom until Nanay calls me. She holds my hand very hard, and in her other hand the stick is clutched just as tightly.

Though it is only two days since Mr. Zamora arrived, new buildings are already growing in the green spaces between the houses on our street. More bamboo has been cut down from the forest, and formed into small squares with banana-leaf roofs. These will be the homes for the new arrivals.

Culion Town feels smaller already, with its gaps filling in. For the first time, it seems less hill and more town, the forest retreating to higher ground. The patch next to the bakery has been trampled completely. Nanay's hand twitches in mine, and I know she is thinking of the seeds we planted. It will never be a butterfly garden now.

Sister Margaritte knocks on all the houses we pass and neighbors join our procession. It is like when we go to funerals, everyone is so silent and downcast. Diwa's new baby is tied to her chest and I try to peek but Diwa has her arms wrapped so close around him all I can see is his forehead. We pass twelve new houses on our street, some fully built and others where the ground has been flattened and bamboo poles lie in stacks on the ground, waiting to be walls.

Capuno and Bondoc are among the men building, and Sister Margaritte gestures for them to join us. At the end of the road we turn left, in the direction of the hospital, and I lose count of the new buildings.

This used to be a stretch of open field, but now trenches for sewage are already dug and I can see the lines of a new street forming. There is no room for gardens and some of the houses share walls. I never knew how much space there was in our town, because all the fields and forests felt necessary. I wonder where the insects that filled the grasses will go.

There is a queue of people snaking down the center of the street, and it is only when Sister Margaritte leads us to the back that I realize the front of the queue is at the hospital, far ahead. There are only a dozen beds there, and they are always full. The examinations must be happening in the waiting room or in Dr. Tomas's office inside his house.

"It shouldn't take that long," says Sister Margaritte to Nanay. "I have to go and help, but I'll see you and Amihan inside."

She walks toward the hospital and we begin our wait. I am good at waiting. I sit down by Nanay's feet and watch the builders, but Nanay can't sit because she doesn't want to have to stand up again in public. She finds it hard with her Touched foot. Diwa's baby wakes with a wail and has to be rocked and fed.

A long time passes, and I see a house sprout up from a patch of earth like a spring. I don't recognize all the builders, but some are obviously Touched. They must have arrived from the Places Outside, maybe on the boat that brought Mr. Zamora. One has a face marked like Nanay's, but he doesn't cover it with a cloth. I suppose that soon this will be a *Leproso* area and no one will have to cover their faces. That will make Nanay happier, even though I will not be with her.

I have to stop thinking this quickly.

After I watch two houses being built and a third starting, I realize we have been waiting a very long time. Even after the sun touches the top of the sky, we have barely moved.

I lie down in the grass and Nanay does not tell me off, even though I am wearing my best dress to meet Mr. Zamora's doctors. She is sweating, and when Sister Margaritte comes back with pails of water, she and Capuno drink a whole one between them. Bondoc and I share because this is one of the things you do to stay Untouched.

"They're going to start walking up the line," says Sister Margaritte softly. "Anyone with obvious signs will be given their identification papers and sent home. Otherwise you will have to wait."

I assume this means me and Bondoc, and Diwa, too, because she is only Touched a little on her foot, so little that it looks like leaf mulch caught between her toes.

"You will need to show them your nose," continues Sister Margaritte to Nanay. Her voice has an apology in it, and I am glad it is not Sister Clara doing this job. "Then you can go home."

Ahead, four men are walking along the line. One of them is Dr. Tomas, whose face is pale and miserable, and another is Mr. Zamora. The other two men in white coats must be his government doctors. His reinforcements. I hope Dr. Tomas reaches us first. The line is moving quicker now, with many people having obvious signs on their faces or arms, and by the time one of the government doctors gets to us, we are nearly at the hospital door anyway.

He is wearing a white cloth mask over his mouth, and white

gloves. He looks at Nanay expectantly and she unwinds her cloth. Her nose does not look good in the daylight, and, without wanting to, I feel embarrassed. For a moment I see her how he must, her cheeks rough with sores and lumps, the folded twists of no-nostrils. Then I shake my head free of these thoughts and see instead her brown eyes, as clear and sharp as a fox's, the smooth brown skin of her long neck, her pulse working quick and visible beneath her ear.

From the pockets of his white coat the stranger draws out a pad and pencil. He beckons for her to step forward and she moves clear of the line, replacing her cloth.

All I can see of the doctor's face are his eyes. They are unlined, and his gloved hands are nimble as they fill out the top form on the pad. He seems young to be a doctor. He hands the pad and the pencil to Nanay and she fills in the boxes marked *name* and *age*. There is a number at the top of the sheet: 0013822.

He rips off the bottom of the form and marks it with a blue-inked stamp. He gives this to her, the number circled. I look down at it with her, and brush the paper with my fingertip. It is rough where other people have signed their names on the paper above it. The doctor gestures for me to hold my hands out and I do. He unfurls my fingers with his pencil, looks at my face and bare legs, then points for me to join the dwindling queue. He moves on to Diwa and her baby without a word.

His silence is catching. It feels as if my tongue is latched to the roof of my mouth. I trip forward to make up the gap between me and the man in front, and Nanay limps with me.

"Not you!" barks a voice. Mr. Zamora is watching us closely. "You—" He points at Nanay. "You have your papers?"

Nanay holds up the piece of paper with the circled number.

"Exactly. So you must proceed home and await the results of your assessment."

"I think the results are fairly clear," says Nanay in a scratchy voice. Maybe her tongue is latched too. Mr. Zamora's lips twitch but it is Dr. Tomas who speaks next.

"Even so, Tala. You can see we don't have the room. It really would be a help if you could wait for Amihan at home."

"I'm still here," says Bondoc from behind me. Capuno is beside him, holding his paper in the snarl of his fist. "I'll walk her home. You can go with Capuno."

Nanay looks from Mr. Zamora to Sister Margaritte to Bondoc with a dazed expression. Then she kneels, although it is painful for her, and hugs me, pinning my arms by my sides.

"I love you, Amihan."

"I love you, too, Nanay," I say, and mean it especially much because of how rude I was in my head when she took off her cloth.

Capuno helps her up and she turns quickly to walk away with him, but not quickly enough for me to miss the tears in her eyes. Bondoc takes my hand in his cavernous palm and we catch up to the queue, which has now moved inside the hospital.

It is hot and smells like it always does, like stale breath and stale water. The examinations are happening in the main room—all the beds are empty and pushed up against the walls. There is no sign of Rosita, Nanay's friend who was admitted last week, or any of the other patients.

There are more men with white face masks and white gloves stationed beside the rails of curtains that normally divide the room. People emerge from behind the curtains and are handed papers by Sister Clara. Sister Margaritte squeezes my shoulder as she goes to join her.

Shortly a doctor with a deep worry line down the center of his forehead calls me forward. Bondoc drops my hand and the room tilts slightly without him mooring me to the floor. I step behind the curtain.

"Name?" says the doctor.

"Amihan."

"Surname?"

I know what this means but don't know the answer, so I give Nanay's name instead.

"Age?"

"Twelve years."

He writes down my name and age on the form, then looks up at me, his eyes crinkling so I know he is smiling despite the face mask.

"So, Amihan Tala. I am Dr. Rodel and I am from Manila. Do you know where that is?"

I nod. Manila is the biggest town in the Places Outside. The place where Mr. Zamora says I will get a job someday, if I am Untouched. It is a very long way from here.

"Nothing I am going to do will hurt, so you mustn't be afraid. I have a granddaughter who is nine, and she doesn't like doctors, even though I, her own *lolo,* am one! Is your *lolo* here at Culion?"

"No." I like him but don't want to show it too much because he is one of Mr. Zamora's doctors.

"Whom do you live with? Was that man with you your *ama*?"

I shake my head and laugh, because Nanay would scrunch up her face and make a disgusted sound if I told her Dr. Rodel thought Bondoc was my father.

"I live with my *nanay,*" I say.

"And where is she?"

"She was sent home with her papers."

"Ah," says Dr. Rodel, and his voice is suddenly serious. "She is a leper, then?"

"We don't use that word," I say, the sentence out before I can draw it back, but Dr. Rodel doesn't seem offended.

"I'm very sorry to have used it, then," he says, eyes creasing again. "I'm afraid I am going to have to keep my mask on, just to be safe. I'll call one of the sisters over, because I'm going to need to check your stomach as well as your legs." He gestures to where they are, and luckily Sister Margaritte is looking, so she is the one who comes over.

"I'm going to need to do a full examination, Sister. Draw the curtains, would you?" says Dr. Rodel. Sister Margaritte pulls the

32

rails into a triangle around the three of us. The light goes paler through the curtain.

Sister Margaritte helps me take off my dress and then wraps a cloth around me so Dr. Rodel can see my skin and check it for marks and numbness. He works quickly, and Sister Margaritte moves the cloth so he can do my stomach, too. It tickles but I don't move. When he is finished, she helps me back into my dress and he puts some cotton on a stick inside my nose and rubs it on my nostril.

"To check for things too small for my old eyes to see," he says as he puts the cotton in a twist of paper. "But it seems your *nanay* has taken very good care of you."

"Yes," I say. I want to ask if this means I can stay with her, but Sister Margaritte has already opened the rails and is leading me toward Bondoc, so I only manage a quick "Thank you."

Dr. Rodel's eyes smile again and then he gestures for Diwa to come forward. Sister Clara hands me a piece of paper. As Bondoc leads me out, Dr. Rodel's crinkling eyes are already drifting to Diwa's Touched toes. Her baby is still crying.

The Results

The paper in my hand is different from Nanay's but the same as Bondoc's. The *Sano* and *Leproso* boxes are empty, and it is unstamped. I suppose that this means they are waiting for the cotton to tell them things Dr. Rodel can't see before deciding what I am.

I know that being Touched comes from tiny specks that travel in your body. That is why Nanay and I must be careful not to drink from the same water or eat from the same spoon, in case these tiny specks go from her to me. But I didn't know that anyone would be able to see them from swabbing my nostril. My nose tingles and I rub it, wondering how I will feel if I am Touched and can stay. How I will feel if I am Untouched but have to go? Both possibilities crouch heavy as demons on my shoulders.

The men are still working in the field. Already I can't remember how it looked without houses on it. It's funny how that happens. I can't remember how Nanay's face looked before her nose folded, or what school was like before Sister Margaritte came. The way things are rewrites the way things were so quickly.

Nanay is fussing around inside the house when we arrive, sweeping up dust from the dirt floor and then re-sweeping it in the other direction. Capuno is watching her with an amused expression on his face.

"Well?"

Bondoc settles down beside his brother to tell them about the government doctors and the curtains drawn around in triangles and the cotton sticks in our nostrils.

"Where did they put the patients?" asks Nanay. "Ami, did you see Rosita?"

"No, the beds were all empty and pushed against the walls."

"That man probably kicked them out into the street," she says, meaning Mr. Zamora.

"So they took swabs?" says Capuno. "What help will that be?"

"For a microscope," says Bondoc. "My doctor said they brought one with them from Manila."

"What's a microscope?" I ask.

"It shows you things up close," says Nanay. "It will tell the doctors if you have the tiny specks that make you Touched."

"I hope I do," says Bondoc bitterly. "I hope I gave them to Mr. Zamora when I stood before him in church."

"Tsk, Bondoc," she says. "You don't know what you are talking about."

"What do your papers look like?" Capuno asks me, and I know he is changing the subject. I show him the paper and he shakes his head. "So now we wait."

We wait for a very long time. A whole evening and morning sky circles over us. Bondoc and Capuno sleep by our fire and in the morning they make us breakfast. We sit inside all day so we don't miss the knock, but soon it is evening again and the moon is in its fullest roundness outside. Nanay, Bondoc, Capuno and I are just sitting down to a meal of rice and salted fish when someone raps on the door.

"Come in," says Nanay.

Dr. Tomas steps inside.

"We were just about to eat," she says, getting up stiffly.

"My apologies, Tala. I have the results for Ami. And you, Bondoc."

"Well?"

"Would you rather I came back?" He looks nervous and I know that it is not good news, but then I don't know what news *could* be fully good.

"No," says Bondoc, who has not stood up and is glaring at Dr. Tomas. "Tell us what your Mr. Zamora has sent you to say."

Dr. Tomas clears his throat and passes two pieces of paper to Nanay and Capuno. "These are your official papers. They confirm you have *Mycobacterium leprae,* and must reside within the *Leproso* areas when they come into force."

"And me?" says Bondoc.

"You are clean," says Dr. Tomas, and holds out another piece of paper. Bondoc stands and snatches it from his hand.

"You even talk like them now," he hisses, and Dr. Tomas drops his eyes.

"And Ami?" says Nanay. I can hear the quiver on her lips.

"I'm so sorry, Tala," says Dr. Tomas. Nanay takes the paper from his hand and scans it. Then she starts to cry.

"Nanay?"

She tries to speak but her whole body is shaking.

"Sister Margaritte will come tomorrow to explain what this means." Dr. Tomas leaves quietly.

Bondoc takes the paper and says, "Oh, Tala."

He passes it to me. Beneath my name and age, above the blue-inked stamp, is a neat cross in a box. Below the box is a single word.

Now I know which I would have preferred. It was not this.

Sano.

Nanay is worn out from crying, so she goes to bed while the rest of us tidy up. When the brothers leave, I am still fizzing with energy. I hover outside our bedroom.

"Nanay?" I can hear her ragged breathing, and sit beside her on the bed. Her back is to me. "I'm sorry," I say.

Her hand reaches behind her and gropes for mine. "Why are you apologizing? This is good news." Another sob grips her throat as she speaks. "You are well, my little girl. Healthy. This is good news."

I can't think of anything to say, so I just sit there until her breaths slow into sleep. I'm not tired at all. My blood feels as if it is filled with little beads of heat. It will be noisy for Nanay if I stay in the house to play, so I collect the racing berries from the garden and go into the street.

My feet take me to the field where we queued. The houses grow like square bushes on either side of the sewage channel. The men have all left and the only light comes from the moon and the hospital. I wonder about going to see if Rosita is there, but I don't want any of the government doctors to see me.

Nanay will be worried if she wakes up and I'm not there. I walk partway up the new street and begin to place one of my racing berries on the threshold of each of the houses as a welcome present. I run out of berries, and begin picking more from a low shrub before I realize it is silly. They probably won't notice the berries. Even if they do, they won't know who they are from, because when they arrive, I will be gone.

My chest aches. It is only by climbing into bed with Nanay and curling my body against the warm scoop of her back that it begins to loosen. I tuck one of the berries into her pocket, and hope that she at least will know it's from me.

The Collector

K *nock!*
My body jumps awake, as if stopping itself falling from a great height.

Knock! Knock! Knock!

Someone is banging on the door. Nanay is already up, her side of the bed cool, uncreasing slowly in her absence. My heart slows as I hear the door creak open and Bondoc's voice.

"Tala, we're going to sort this out. Come with me."

"What do you—" starts Nanay.

"Come now. Sister Margaritte's got us an appointment."

"Appointment? For what?"

"For sorting this out. Let's go!"

"I can't leave Ami."

"I'll come with you," I call, slipping on my sandals and hurrying through to where Nanay is standing in the doorway. Bondoc's hand is on her cheek and he drops it hurriedly, though I have seen his hand on her cheek and hers on his many times before when they thought I wasn't looking.

Nanay turns to me. "I don't even know where we're going—"

"I'll explain on the way," says Bondoc, stepping back and holding out his hands to us. "We have to be there by nine, or he won't see us."

"He?"

"Come on, Tala!" Capuno emerges from his brother's shadow. "We have to leave now."

Capuno is more sensible than Bondoc, and him urging Nanay seems to decide it. She wraps her face and picks up her stick, and I close the door behind us, hurrying to keep up with Bondoc's strides.

We are following the steps we took yesterday, and the ones I took last night—down our street, through the field that is now houses, toward the hospital. I scan the doorsteps for berries, but they are gone. Every one, gone. As we walk, Nanay hisses at Bondoc to explain, and Bondoc tells her we are to see Mr. Zamora, to put our case to him.

"Our case?"

"For Ami to stay."

Nanay's hand clenches mine, and I feel her slowing until it is like walking through mud and I am almost dragging her.

40

"I don't want to see that man."

"I know," says Capuno softly. "But it is worth a try, yes?"

Nanay stops and takes in a great hiccup of a breath.

"Yes," I answer for her.

Bondoc squeezes my shoulder, his hand huge and heavy and warm. Nanay nods, and we keep walking.

We walk past the berryless houses and the queuing people at the hospital to Dr. Tomas's house, a neat square built on two floors with wrought-iron balconies at the windows. Bondoc knocks twice on the wooden door, and Sister Margaritte opens it.

"Come, quickly. It's nearly five past."

Inside is cool, the floor stone, like in church. There are framed pictures on the lemon-yellow walls, and the first room we pass is filled with piles and piles of paper, with Dr. Tomas sitting on a low chair, leaning on his knees to write in a large book. He looks up as Sister Margaritte ushers us on, closing the door on the piled-paper room. The door has a small square sign saying DR. TOMAS, hung lopsidedly.

"So he's a guest in his own house now?" says Nanay, and Capuno shushes her while Bondoc snorts. We are led up the stairs, which creak ominously as we climb. Sister Margaritte brings us to a stop on the narrow landing.

We all crowd around the door. It is white except for a small square patch of unpainted wood in the middle. This must have been where Dr. Tomas's sign used to be. Above it, a large sign hanging on a nail reads:

MR. ZAMORA
AUTHORIZED REPRESENTATIVE
TO THE DIRECTOR OF HEALTH

It is in the same red lettering as the notices. I try to swallow the lump that rises in my throat as Sister Margaritte knocks.

"Enter."

She turns the handle.

The room is full of color. The walls are flecked like the church's stained glass, with reds and purples and greens and blues, as if vines of *gumamela* flowers have threaded up them. But it is not flowers that crowd the room—it is butterflies. Butterflies lined up like schoolchildren, or an army, in neat rows.

"What is this?" Bondoc growls.

"Ah, do you like my collection? I go nowhere without them," says Mr. Zamora, unfolding slow as a nightmare from behind a low wooden desk. He is wearing a pink tie drawn tight enough to butt against the apple of his throat when he talks. "They are dear as children to me. Rhopalocera. Or as you may know them—"

"We know *what* they are," interrupts Bondoc. "Why are they here, like this?"

"I am a lepidopterist," says Mr. Zamora.

"We don't use that word," says Bondoc warningly.

"A lep-i-dopterist, Bondoc," says Sister Margaritte. "Not 'leper.'"

"Oh." Bondoc folds in on himself, seeming to lose height.

"Yes," says Mr. Zamora with a smirk, thin fingers spreading

to indicate the walls. "Or to put it in terms you may understand, I collect and study butterflies."

"These are all dead?" I ask, though I know they must be, to be so still. The colors of the wings ripple like fish underwater.

"No, I trained them to settle like that," Mr. Zamora sneers. "Yes, of course they're dead. I breed them, hatch them, pin them . . ."

"You breed them just to die?" says Nanay.

"So that I may study them," Mr. Zamora repeats, raking his eyes across her scarf as he sits back down, pointedly scraping his chair back and away from her. "Is this why you've come? To question me about butterflies?"

"No," says Nanay coolly. "But it is interesting to know."

"We've come," says Capuno hurriedly, breaking the bristling silence, "to discuss your plans to remove the children—"

"The *government's* plans," interrupts Mr. Zamora.

"You are their authorized representative, are you not?" snaps Bondoc, who is done shrinking. "Or did I misunderstand the sign you've hung on Dr. Tomas's door?"

"I am indeed the government's representative." Mr. Zamora narrows his eyes. "And you would do well to reflect that in your tone."

Capuno steps between Bondoc and the desk, pulling from his pocket a carefully folded piece of paper. "I have here a petition, signed by the parents of all the Untouched children who are to be taken, and plenty of us without children too. We request—"

"We *demand*—" interjects Bondoc.

"That you reconsider your plans to relocate the children to the Places Outside."

"Places outside?" Mr. Zamora's voice is mocking, his thick eyebrows rising toward his thin hair.

"To the next island," says Capuno calmly. "To Coron."

"I see," says Mr. Zamora, obviously amused. My skin is as hot as if he were making fun of me.

"We feel it must be possible for the children to stay on Culion, if not in the town itself. Perhaps things can remain as they are, or perhaps they can keep to the areas you have devised and see their parents in a monitored environment. Surely anything is preferable to separating families." Capuno was a teacher before he came here, a good one, I imagine, with his straight back and clear voice. "So, here it is."

He unfolds the piece of paper and holds it out toward Mr. Zamora.

He does not reach for it for what feels like a moon age. His face is placid, like a lake hiding the snapping log of a crocodile. Eventually Sister Margaritte takes the paper and places it on the desk in front of him. It is a tangle of names. People have written up the margins and between the other words. I feel the first bright start of hope. Surely he can't ignore so many names?

"Read it, sir," says Sister Margaritte. "Please."

"I hope you say your prayers in a more persuasive tone, Sister," says Mr. Zamora, giving the same hard emphasis to the last word as she did to "sir." He lets out an exaggerated sigh, and leans forward slightly to open the top drawer of the desk.

He takes out a pair of tweezers and lays them carefully by the petition. Then he takes out a glass disk with a wooden handle attached and puts this next to the tweezers, nudging it this way and that to make them all line up neatly. Like soldiers, or schoolchildren, or pinned butterflies. Then he closes the drawer. He does all these things with an infinite slowness that makes my skin prickle and crawl.

With one hand he picks up the tweezers, pincers the top corner of the petition and lifts it, keeping his long arm extended. With his other hand he picks up the handle of the glass disk, and peers through it. His eye bulges huge through the glass, flicking back and forth as he reads aloud:

"We the undersigned write in protest to point four of Article Fifteen, as decreed by Government Representative Mr. Zamora. We request that persons under eighteen be afforded the same right as those over eighteen: namely, that the Director of Health authorizes this person to remain on Culion, on the condition they stay within the *Sano* areas. Limited trespass may be made into *Leproso* areas under authorized supervision." It is horrible to hear the words, quoted from the signs stuck up on every street, spoken out loud, especially in Mr. Zamora's faintly amused tone.

"We feel that this is the kindest and most tenable way to temper the already traumatic effects of forced separation, without resorting to forced migration. Signed ..." Mr. Zamora looks up from the petition. "Seemingly everyone on this sorry rock."

"Not quite everyone," says Nanay. She had been standing so still it felt as if I were holding hands with a statue, or a tree, but now she reaches forward and plucks a pen from the inkwell on Mr. Zamora's desk.

"Don't—" exclaims Mr. Zamora, but Nanay has already ripped the petition away from the tweezers, leaving a shred behind between the glinting pincers. She scrawls her name in a tiny piece of space, then puts the petition back down on the desk, jabbing the pen back into the inkwell so little black spots spray everywhere.

"There. *Now* everyone on this *sorry rock* has signed it," Nanay hisses. She is breathing hard, her scarf flaring in and out. Behind her, Bondoc is looking at her as if she is as wondrous and terrifying as a tiger.

Mr. Zamora is staring at her too, but as if he has seen a ghost. His arms are raised as if he still holds the petition, the fragment quivering in the tweezers. His skin is pale as paper, his puffy lips mouth wordlessly. His gaze flickers from Nanay to the ink spots that are blooming across the square piles of papers, across Nanay's scarf. He whimpers like a kicked dog, and looks down at the spreading black on his pink tie.

"Mr. Zamora?" says Sister Margaritte.

He whispers something.

"Pardon?" she says.

"Out," he says, quiet as a hiccup. "Get out."

"But, sir, you haven't given us an answer," says Capuno, stepping forward.

Mr. Zamora reels back, knocking over the chair and drawing himself up jerkily.

"Don't come near me!"

Capuno stops mid-implore.

"You want an answer?" Mr. Zamora turns his back on us and opens the drawer of the dresser he has stumbled against. He takes out a small bottle and scouring pad, then squirts the clear liquid from the bottle onto the ink on his tie. A sharp smell prickles my nose, like the tang of the hospital. While he speaks, he begins to scrub.

"The answer is no. No matter how many petitions, how many signatures, no matter how much you lepers and your offspring want a different answer, it will still be no."

"But—" starts Capuno.

"And you'll be wanting a reason, as if the reason is not clear enough!" Mr. Zamora is not looking at any of us, which I am glad about because I don't want him to see me cry. "We want to end this disease. And do you know how we kill a disease? We stop ... it ... breeding." He stops scrubbing his tie and puts some of the clear liquid on his hands, then begins to scour his palms. "We stop it multiplying. And to do that, we must keep clean." His palms are scrubbed raw.

Sister Margaritte touches Nanay on the shoulder and we all begin to back away toward the door. Mr. Zamora continues speaking into his hands, which have started to bleed.

"We stop it cleanly in its tracks. We take the clean ones, and give them a clean life. Surely you must agree that is important above all things. Take these butterflies," he says, gesturing at the walls. "They have never known disease, or danger. I even give them a clean death—is that not a kindness? They are beautiful. Clean. Untouched by the world."

Sister Margaritte opens the door and we hurry out. Before she closes it, I look back at Mr. Zamora, still scrubbing, surrounded by the rainbow patchwork of dead butterflies. He looks up, finally. He is panting, his eyes wild.

"We will make history of lepers," he says, "and a museum of this island."

Sister Margaritte slams the door.

My hands are shaking, and even Bondoc trembles as we leave Dr. Tomas's house. I hear Dr. Tomas asking Sister Margaritte what happened, but she only shakes her head and walks past us all without a word. She takes the path down toward the sea, toward church, and I know she is going to pray.

The rest of us walk in our own little bubble of quiet past the hospital and its queue of people, past the new houses, all the way home. Nanay is limping heavily, leaning as much on me as she does on her stick. Bondoc hovers, but she does not fall.

At home, I boil water and steep gingerroot. I huddle next to Nanay as we drink.

"He's sick," says Capuno finally.

"We knew that already," rumbles Bondoc.

"No, *really* sick," says his brother. "Did you see how he laid the tweezers and magnifying glass out? Such precision. And how regimented those butterflies are?"

Lepidopterist, I think, rolling the word out over my silent tongue. *Lep-i-dop-ter-ist.* The beats drift softly up and down, like butterfly kisses.

"And how he reacted when I got near him," says Nanay in a small voice. "He wasn't just disgusted, he was scared."

"We should report him," says Bondoc.

"To whom?" sighs Capuno.

"The government that sent him!"

"But they are in agreement," says Capuno. "He is acting on their behalf."

"Then why the petition?" Nanay says sharply. "Why give us that hope?"

"Because it was worth it, wasn't it?" says Capuno. "To try everything?"

She does not answer him. I am not sure either.

The Boat

Because these are the last days Nanay and I will be together—until I have lived six years without her and can come back to live in the *Sano* areas—we decide to try to do fun things but feel so sad it doesn't really work. Six years is half my life so far, every other day lived without her. It feels impossible.

Most of the fun things only make it feel more impossible. We plant the garden with vegetables I will not see grow. We fix the wickerwork on chairs that will need reweaving by the time I get back from Coron. I say "we," but Nanay spends most of her time wincing when she thinks I'm not looking. She finds it hard to kneel, to grip the spade, to scatter the seeds. She does not even try to help with the chairs. How will she do any of these things without me?

It is only now, when I am about to leave her, that I realize how much I help her. Like a tide coming in, it has crept up on us, me doing more with each passing year: I help her dress, cook, clean. But if Nanay is worried, she does not show it.

Every day she insists we go to our favorite beach for lunch, though it is a long walk. It has the whitest sand, and despite there being a small harbor with a pier nearby, none of the fishermen launch their boats from this side of the rocks, so often we are alone. I think of our visit to Mr. Zamora, of his fear, and, most of all, of the butterflies.

"Why does he keep them like that?" I ask on the day after our meeting.

"To make himself feel powerful," says Nanay. "To make himself feel clever."

"And because they are beautiful, maybe?"

"Do you think it is right to trap a thing because you think it is beautiful? To kill it? I love butterflies too, you know." Nanay swallows. "Your *ama* planted flowers to bring them to our house. Two summers I saw them, just before the rains. They'd cover the house like leaves, like …" She scrunches up her face, trying to find the right word. "Like petals—orange and blue and white. They stayed for a whole week one year. It was enough to see them for a few days alive. Better than seeing them forever but dead."

I am barely breathing as she says this. She hardly ever talks about my father, has never mentioned details of their life together. A house covered in butterflies—I try to picture it.

"Is that why you want to bring the butterflies here?" I say. "To the patch by the bakery?"

Nanay blinks, as if coming around from a daydream. "It was a long time ago. And that patch is gone now, built on." Nanay looks me straight in the eye. "My point was, Mr. Zamora does not collect them because he likes them. They're just specimens to him. A project. Something to know a lot about because it makes him feel clever."

"Your butterfly house—"

"A world ago. Come, let's eat." Her voice shakes, and though I dream of a forest with a house at its heart, pulsing with wings, I do not ask her about it again.

On our fourth day of lunch at the beach, we haunch in the lapping waves and watch for shrimp. The tide is coming in and they arrive like a flock of birds, tiny and blue-white. Nanay sieves them from the water with a piece of cotton. I scan for the scuttle of crabs, and one nips me on the toe before I can catch it. Some of the older boys from school are playing ball nearby, and they point and laugh as I hop around, rubbing my toe.

Nanay offers to swap jobs and I manage to collect a basketful of shrimp while she gets several small crabs, young enough for their shells to be soft. We dig out a fire pit and Nanay lights the wood she has brought from home.

She fries the shrimp with a little oil and garlic root in her shallow metal basin. It heats quickly, and when it is hot enough, she adds the crab.

"This was my mother's," she says, tapping the basin. "It was her mother's wedding present to her. She was going to give it to me at my wedding but then I was brought here. So she sent it to me."

The sadness in her voice has many layers. I used to ask Nanay about her family constantly, but it always made her shrink inside herself, or snap at me, so I stopped. I don't know how to draw her out of it because I feel sad too, so I make myself useful instead and fetch banana leaves for us to eat off, and straight sticks to pick out the shrimp and crab.

The crab shells are crisp, the insides cooked into a lovely melting lightness, and we eat them whole. The shrimp are so small they jump from the oil as it spits. I salvage some from the beach and am able to make Nanay laugh by pulling faces when the sand crunches between my teeth. We don't really talk as we eat, so it is barely noon when we swallow the last crab, split down the middle. Nanay is tired and her foot hurts, so she lies down in the shade with her face cloth on to stop sand going in her eyes and nostrils.

I watch the boys kicking the ball. The tallest, Datu, will also be leaving for Coron, and I wonder about going to talk to him, but he sticks out his tongue when he sees me looking. I am good at playing on my own, so I don't mind.

First I cover the fire pit, because the wind is blowing the flames too close to the tree line. Then I pretend the sea is acid and that I must build trenches to stop it touching us. I dig with my hands as fast as I can, but it becomes harder when I get below the soft, loose sand and reach the harder, damp stuff. The tide is creeping closer and I want to ask Nanay to move farther up to stop it touching her, but I know she will say I am being silly. It is just a game.

Eventually I can't stop the water lapping her feet—she can't feel things on her soles anymore, which is another thing being Touched means for her—so I sit beside her and watch the sea instead. It seems to hold more light than the sun is giving it, as if there is a second sun or a mirror below its surface, so the whole ocean dazzles at the sky. It is almost too bright to look at, and I am squinting when I notice the shape far out at sea.

At first I think it is a rock or shadows cast by the waves, but it moves closer and grows larger the longer I watch. It is soon only a Bondoc-stone's-throw away, and the voices become audible and the smell of many bodies catches on the wind. The boys stop their game, picking up their ball and taking off toward the town.

I have seen boats before, but never one this big, nor one so full of people. It is sitting so low in the water that the sea's shimmer makes it look as if the passengers are walking on water. It is rectangular, formed of planks of wood nailed together, and the varnish gleams wetly in the sunlight. It has been built in a rush, just like the houses, I think.

When I look at the people, they seem unfinished too. I have seen Touched people arriving before, of course, but usually one at a time, brought by silent men on small boats. There are so many here, and some are missing limbs or noses. There is a man with what looks like an overgrown baby strapped to his back with stained cloth, but when he turns, I see it is not a baby but an old woman. I can tell by the shape of her body pressing against the cloth that she does not have her legs. Rosita has no legs either, but she is carried in a wheeled chair with a cloth draped over, not bundled on someone's back like an infant. It doesn't seem right.

The boat is now only a me-stone's-throw away, and it is so long only the front can tuck itself alongside the wooden pier. There are probably a hundred passengers, no more than a church service's worth, but I feel I have never seen so many Touched before. From what I can tell, there is not a person there without visible signs. As Mr. Zamora said, they must have come from all over the Places Outside. I wonder how they must be feeling, crammed in among strangers with only one thing in common—the only thing that matters to the government and people like Mr. Zamora.

"You, child—come and help moor us!" The man steering the boat has Touched sores on his arms. They are open and weeping, and Dr. Tomas told us that means they're infectious and warned us against going near, but I don't want to be rude.

There is a girl about my age squashed up against the side facing me. Her nose is folded and she is watching me carefully. Her eyes are bright with fear, like a caged rabbit's. I want her first impression of Culion to be good. I look at Nanay, who is still sleeping, undisturbed by the stale smell of unwashed bodies and the sounds of voices speaking in unfamiliar dialects, and walk to the pier.

The boatman throws the rope. I catch the heavy, stinking end and wrap it around a post the way Capuno taught me. I don't think it will hold very well but I can't stay close to the smell for long enough to double-knot it. I step back and the captain climbs up and places a wooden plank across the gap.

"Did the government man send you?" His voice is rough and clipped.

I shake my head.

"Typical," he mutters. "They're in a rush to get us here and no one to greet us!"

"Ami?" Nanay is sitting up, shielding her eyes from the sun. I watch her see me, then the boat, then the people. She looks at the people for a long while, many breaths in and out through her nostrils. Then she is up and running toward me, fumbling her face cloth over her mouth and landing heavily on her Touched foot.

"Ami, away! Get away from there!"

Many people turn to watch her hobbling, and I feel bad for them. I can tell she is afraid. Bondoc says you can catch fear easier than becoming Touched, and some of the arrivals are looking nervously around for what has scared this wild-eyed woman enough to make her run on her Touched foot.

"Get away, I said!" She arrives panting, the boatman watching her with amusement clear on his face.

"What's the problem, lady?"

Nanay is already pulling me, barging past the passengers who have disembarked and drawing me close to her.

"Nanay?" I start hesitantly, but her face is furious. She has my upper arm in a viselike hold and is heading back toward home, although her stick and her metal basin are still on the beach.

I look back over my shoulder and see that the arrivals are still standing on the beach, probably waiting for someone to tell them what to do. Halfway up the hill we pass the boys and Datu says, "Was it them? From the Places Outside?" But Nanay does not slow down to let me answer.

As soon as we are home, Nanay wheels me around roughly to face her.

"What do you think you were doing?" she shouts at me through the cloth. "Did you really think I wouldn't notice?"

"Notice what—"

"It's that stupid petition, putting ideas in your head!"

"I don't—"

"Don't play innocent with me. I know what you were doing! You took me to the beach today, you knew they were coming, you knew I'd fall asleep—"

"We've been to the beach every day, Nanay." I follow her with my eyes as she paces. I have never seen her so angry.

"And if I hadn't woken up, you would have . . . would have . . ." Her breath is coming in big gulps like a fish out of water.

"Nanay," I try again. "I don't know what you are saying. But I'm sorry for upsetting you."

She turns so sharply I think she is going to continue shouting, but then she crouches before me. I hear her inhale deeply but she doesn't speak. Her eyes, pinched by worry lines, are no longer angry. She sinks back onto the floor and wraps her arms around her knees, resting her chin on them. She is shrunken, whereas only moments before rage had grown her big as Bondoc.

I sit down and rest my chin on my knees too, to show that I am happy to wait for her to tell me what is wrong. Finally she unwinds her face cloth.

"You really weren't trying to be near those people on purpose? The ones with open sores?"

I am more confused than ever. "No. I was just helping them moor the boat, like Capuno taught me."

Nanay's head sinks down and her shoulders shake, so I crawl forward and wrap my arms as far around her as they can go. "I thought you wanted to be near them. I thought you wanted to catch it."

"Catch it?"

Nanay's face is already swollen from crying. "Those people, their sores were undressed. It would have been easy to . . . catch this." She gestures at her nose.

"Oh." I can't think of anything else to say. Nanay takes my hands gently and looks me straight in the eyes.

"Ami, I believe you. But I do not believe you haven't tried to think of a way to stay. I love you, Ami, and that means that I want a better life for you. It is a blessing that you have stayed with me so long, and I want you to stay forever. But I will not be here forever." Her voice falters. "This disease is more terrible than you can understand. Mr. Zamora is right. There is no future on an island of lepers."

I want to correct her use of the word, but my mouth has stopped working.

"So you must go. It is for the best. You will be all right in the Places Outside. You are the kindest girl I know." She reaches into her pocket and pulls out the berry. "Did you give me this?"

I nod.

"Then I must give you something. That is how love works, yes?"

"Yes. Giving and receiving."

"Exactly. Not give, give, give, like that God-of-the-Church demands." She looks around her and then claps a hand to her forehead. "I left the basin!"

"I didn't want to remind you when you were angry."

She laughs softly. "I was quite scary, wasn't I? I got that from my mother, too. Well, let's fetch it."

I jump up. "I'll go. You left your stick."

She blinks around her as if she has just noticed, and then nods slowly. I know what she wants to say next but is embarrassed to because she shouted at me. So I say it for her.

"I won't go near any of those people. I promise."

She nods again. "Careful of the oil. It may still be hot."

That is her way of saying "Be careful of everything."

The Butterfly House

When I get home, Sister Margaritte is with Nanay, and they both rise from the floor when I walk in.

"There you are, Amihan," says Nanay briskly, wiping her eyes with one hand and taking her stick with the other. "I was just about to come and find you."

"Hello, Ami," says Sister Margaritte. "I'm sorry for interrupting your day with your mother, but there were some important details I had to tell her. I'm sure she will fill you in."

She reaches out her hand and I put down the basin to take it. "God bless you, child. I am sure Coron will be a wonderful adventure."

Her hand is warm and dry, her fingernails spotless as usual, small and pink as shells. My own hand looks dirty and clumsy in her grasp. I wonder if it is prayers that make her hands like that.

"Thank you, Sister Margaritte," I say. She nods her head and leaves.

Nanay beckons me over. I sit on her crossed legs and she wraps her arms around me, my spine pressing against her chest so I am cocooned between her chin and lap. I try to still the moment in my mind. I will be bigger when I see her next time—I want to remember being held like this.

"Sister Margaritte was sent to fetch you," she says in a quiet voice. "Segregation is starting tomorrow, and Mr. Zamora wanted all the Untouched children taken to Coron tonight. But Sister Margaritte argued with him and he agreed you could all go tomorrow instead."

"Tomorrow?" My body jerks involuntarily but Nanay holds me tightly.

"We mustn't think of it as only a day left, but rather a day extra," she continues, and I can tell Sister Margaritte has told her what to say. "We will be able to write to each other, and I will write to you every day until we see each other again."

"But that is six years!"

"Not quite," she says, speaking faster. "Your birthday is in four months, so really it is only five years and four months. That's . . ." She scrunches up her face, and I know the numbers in her head are flicking. Nanay is good at numbers, says she can see them, clear as if she were writing them out. "One thousand, nine hundred and forty-five days, or thereabouts. So I will write you one thousand, nine hundred and forty-five—or thereabouts—letters."

I think she thinks these numbers make it feel easier for me, but they don't have the same comfort as they do for her. So many days have to pass, starting sooner than I ever guessed. Starting tomorrow.

"I know it sounds like a lot, but Sister Margaritte says it's fewer than the number of steps we take to the beach and back—that isn't so far, is it?"

"So each day is a step?"

"Exactly." Her voice is calm again. She kisses the back of my head. "A step bringing us closer together."

Though they aren't her words—Nanay would never put things like this, so sweetly and softly, so like Sister Margaritte—they do help. I print one thousand, nine hundred and forty-five into my brain alongside all the other important numbers: mine and Nanay's birthdays, the number of brass lights in church, Nanay's identification number.

"I'll write to you, too," I say. Though I've never sent anyone a letter before, I'm sure I will work it out. Maybe people in the orphanage will help me. We sit thinking our separate thoughts for a while. I am mainly wondering what Nanay is thinking, and about how tomorrow is sooner than I know what to do with.

"Do you want some dinner?" Nanay says eventually. I shake my head. "Want to catch some stars?"

The wall opposite is dim and I hadn't even noticed.

"Yes."

We unfurl ourselves stiffly and I help Nanay to her feet. She fetches the sheet from our bed and we go outside. Noise from the new street and the tavern is carrying on the wind, but I take her to my sun patch and the trees muffle the sound. She spreads the sheet on the ground and we both lie down.

"What's it like, crossing the sea?" I have only ever been out on Bondoc's boat, barely past the reef that circles the island.

"It is a long time since I came," says Nanay thoughtfully. "But it felt a bit like being rocked in a cradle. Everything is unsteady at sea."

"But I'll be safe?"

"Yes, the sea channel here is calm. All the currents pull toward land in both directions—I remember when I arrived, the boat seemed to bring itself in."

"So if I fell out, I'd float back to Culion?"

"Don't get ideas," laughs Nanay softly.

The stars are set gently against their spread of deep, dark blue. I try to section off the sky and count them, but every time I focus on one star to start counting outward from it, my eye gets drawn to another and I lose my place. Every so often one falls across the sky and Nanay or I point and say "Catch!" The person who says it first wins the star. I am much better than Nanay normally, but this time I only win by three.

When it gets cold, we go inside. I don't want to fall asleep, because when I wake up, it will be tomorrow, and Nanay seems to feel the same, because she suggests we tell stories.

She tells me about an island with black sands and white

forests where giants live and shake the earth, and that is where the tsunamis start. It is a good story and I have to think hard of one that will be as good. So I tell her about a place where the ground is upside down and people walk around attached by their feet, the sky opening like a mouth below them. They can never sleep because they will lose their grip on the ground and fall into the clouds.

"That's very clever," she says. "May I tell you one more?"

She shuffles onto her side and props herself up on her elbow. "Once there was a girl, and she was in love with a boy. He was in love with her, too, but he was very sick and told her they could not be together. He moved to a small hut many miles away, but the girl followed him. She told him she would look after him. They wanted to be married but were too young and he was too sick. So they lived together anyway, and he began to get better.

"They were very happy for many years. They made the hut beautiful by painting the roof blue and training red *gumamela* flowers to climb the walls. They're beautiful open flowers with thin tongues trumpeting from the center. Once a year the butterflies came and made them flicker like fire. You could see their house from the top of the surrounding hills, because of the blue roof and red flowers. That's how they were found.

"Eventually the girl's family went looking for her. When they saw the hut from the top of the hill, they waited until it was dark. Then they crept down, overpowered the boy and took the girl back home. She was very sad and the sadness crept into her blood. Soon she was as sick as the boy. Her family blamed him, but she knew it was because she was heartbroken. They sent her to an island where all the heartbroken people live, and she thought she would die without ever being happy again. But she was wrong.

"The boy had given her a gift before she was taken, and now she found it growing inside her. Her belly grew round and soon the gift was ready. From her body came a beautiful and wondrous breeze, smelling sweet as rain. She named it Amihan, after the winds that bring the monsoon, and so are life-giving. The breeze gave the girl new life, and made her happy for many years, until it was time for it to move on. Even after the breeze went out into the wide world of the Places Outside, it left enough love for a lifetime."

I wait the right amount of silence before speaking. "But, Nanay, you won't have to wait a lifetime. I'll be back in one thousand, nine hundred and forty-five days. Or thereabouts."

Nanay laughs sadly.

"Was the house yours and Ama's? The butterfly house?"

"Yes. It was beautiful."

I can see it clearly from above, like a bird might. The blue roof, the fiery walls. "Is Ama all right now?"

Nanay rolls onto her back so I can't see her face anymore. "I don't know if he stayed better."

It clicks into place. "He was Touched?"

Nanay puts her arm across her eyes. "Yes."

"What was he like?"

Nanay hesitates. "I don't know how to sum him up. It's hard, isn't it? Describing a person in only words, when they can hold whole worlds in them." She swallows. "He was short. He always cut his hair unevenly. His hands were rough. He was the kindest man I've ever known."

"I wish I had met him."

"You are so like him—your smile, your eyes. Your kindness. You are my world now."

I find her hand. We breathe together in the darkness.

The Going

When I wake, there is a small bundle beside me, and with a pang I realize Nanay has packed for me. I sit on my bed for a long time, looking at the room I have spent every night in since I was born. Notches in the doorframe mark my height, from when I was just able to stand to last year's birthday. I wonder how tall I will be when Nanay next measures me. Probably bigger than her—she is not very high.

Nanay sticks her head into the room.

"There you are," she says in a too-bright voice that means she is putting on a brave face. "I made breakfast."

We eat fruit in our scrubby garden, but it is hard to swallow.

I want this part to be over, though I don't want to leave. I don't think the being-gone will be as bad as the going.

Sister Margaritte arrives just as we are finishing our mango halves. Nanay goes rigid and says, "Wipe your face, Ami."

I bite my lip so hard I taste the tang of blood. There must be a way of staying. I wish I had thought harder about it, knew what to do. Nanay hands me my bundle. I can feel hard edges inside and she says, "Your present is in there, like I promised. *Habilin,* for safekeeping until we see each other again."

The parting words are coming, and she is drawing out the sentences to delay it, the way she does when she goes to see friends in the hospital who will not be going home. Sister Margaritte leads us outside.

I keep my back straight and my eyes facing forward. There is an open cart outside with a driver—another stranger—and five other children in it, seated along the sides. They all have bundles with them too. Datu is there, and two girls from school, but most of our class are not. Diwa's baby is not there either.

"A cart?" says Nanay. "Are we not walking them to the harbor?"

"They are to be taken to the new port. The . . ." Sister Margaritte wrinkles her nose. "The *Sano* port. It's north from here, through the forest."

"I see." Nanay chokes on the words. Then she clears her throat and bends to hold me.

"Be good. Be polite. Make yourself useful."

"I will, Nanay."

She hugs me tightly. "Make me proud. Make friends. I'll write to you."

She nods at Sister Margaritte, who looks as sad as I feel.

"See you in one thousand, nine hundred and forty-five days," I say.

"One thousand, nine hundred and forty-*four* days," she corrects. "Or thereabouts."

I climb up and Sister Margaritte sits beside the driver. The horses start walking.

"Wait!"

Bondoc is thundering down the road, Capuno hurrying behind. I move to the back of the cart and each of the brothers reaches up in turn to hug me.

Bondoc whispers into my ear, "I will take care of her, Ami. Segregation or no, I'll visit as much as possible. And I will take care of you, as best I can. I will write to check on you, and visit when you are settled."

He lets go and jumps from the cart.

As the horses start again, Nanay kisses both hands and blows the kisses to me. I catch them fast as falling stars and pocket them. Bondoc puts his arm over Nanay's shoulder and I know he will keep his promise, even if he can only rarely come from the *Sano* area. This should make it better, a little. It should.

They wave until the cart turns off the street. My arms and legs feel heavy; blood is roaring in my ears. My fingers tingle and I clench them into the bundle. I can feel from the size and weight that it's Nanay's metal cooking basin. I know it is the most precious thing she had, and all because I gave her a dried-up berry.

The littlest boy, Kidlat, is sniffling. He can barely be older than five, and no one goes to comfort him, so I shuffle carefully toward him and put my arms around him until he stops crying. His small warmth anchors me. We collect three more children: Tekla and two Igmes (one tall, one short), all girls I know from school but who don't talk to me. At every door there is a mother or father or both, crying and kissing them goodbye. It is hard to watch, so I keep my eyes closed until the cart starts moving again.

Our final stop is at Dr. Tomas's house. The doctor is standing outside looking tired, surrounded by boxy suitcases. Sister Margaritte climbs down to greet him, and for a moment I think the doctor is coming instead of Mr. Zamora. But then the butterfly collector looms out of the house wearing a white straw hat and holding a glass case a bit smaller than a suitcase. The sun glints off it, throwing sharp points of light that make stars shoot across my eyes, but as Mr. Zamora carefully slides it onto the front seat of the cart next to the driver, we all crane to look.

Inside are rows and rows of wooden sticks, set horizontally through holes in the glass like the rungs of a ladder. Dangling from each of these sticks are what look like dried leaves, ten or more on each. They sway as Mr. Zamora sets the case down, as though they may drop.

"Back!" barks Mr. Zamora, and Kidlat starts to whimper again. "Don't touch it!"

"What is it?" asks Lilay, one of the older girls.

"They are chrysalises," says Mr. Zamora.

"Chrisa-what?"

"Caterpillar cases," says Sister Margaritte. "Where they go to change into butterflies."

"Indeed. And they are very delicate. If you touch them . . ." Mr. Zamora drags his gaze over each of us. I look down. "You will be punished. It is not ideal having to transport them in this . . . rustic manner."

"You could use the harbor here," says the driver. "Be kinder to allow the parents to wave their children off. Most of them have never been in a boat before."

"That is a *Leproso* port now," snaps Mr. Zamora. "The north-easterly harbor will be where *Sano* transportation is organized."

"Perhaps you would like more time?" says Sister Margaritte, half sharply, half hopefully. "Wait until the roads are laid, and a less *rustic* form of transport can be brought from the Places Outside?"

"And spend another day in Culion Leper Colony?" He smiles as she flinches. "I think I made my feelings on that quite clear, Sister." He wheels around to Dr. Tomas. "When you're ready, Doctor!"

Dr. Tomas jumps and begins loading the rest of the boxes and suitcases into the cart. There are five brown boxes in all, two up front with Mr. Zamora and three at the back, each with holes pricked in the top to let in air. I bring my head down to listen but there is no sound.

Mr. Zamora oversees the loading as if the doctor is a servant. When the luggage is loaded and the floor of the cart is so tightly packed we can barely move our feet, Mr. Zamora pulls a spotless white handkerchief from his pocket and covers the handrail he uses to pull himself onto the front seat. He lets the handkerchief drop into the dust and slowly lifts the glass case onto his lap, setting the chrysalises swinging.

Sister Margaritte goes to climb up next to him but Mr. Zamora holds his hand up, right in her face. "No need, Sister. I'll take them from here."

Sister Margaritte draws herself up to her fullest height. "I have cared for these children for years. I'm not about to let them go with someone they barely know."

"You have no choice, Sister," says Mr. Zamora in a not-sorry voice. "Your new charges will be arriving soon. You'll have a whole school of leper children to worry about. And besides, I know what I am doing." Mr. Zamora twists around in his seat. "The government has put me in charge of seeing to it that all you bright young people get a good start in your new lives. I'll be running the orphanage."

His lips peel back from his teeth in an attempt at a comforting smile. Kidlat's mouth quivers and he nuzzles closer to me. Sister Margaritte hesitates, and steps back. She looks as if she has lost a tug-of-war, her shoulders drooping. She climbs into the back of the cart and hugs each of us.

"You should be there by sunset," she says, sniffling. "I've

been to Coron. It's a friendly place. I am sure you will be happy there."

I search her face but she seems to be telling the truth. Maybe we *will* be happy there, even without our families. Nanay once told me a story about a town run by children. They stayed young forever and it was a joy-filled place.

I hold on to this shining thought as Mr. Zamora says, "Let's get on with it, then."

I watch Sister Margaritte watching us go. She has one hand on Dr. Tomas's shoulder and they are both perfectly still. As we round a corner, she is as small as my forearm, a doll dressed in black. The horses pull us out of Culion, past all the houses, the hospital and church, out underneath a new sign set high over the road between two poles:

CULION LEPER COLONY
RESTRICTED AREA

Mr. Zamora doffs his hat at it, lets out a long breath and inhales an even longer one.

"Free, children! Fresh air from here on."

The Escape

W e only stop when someone needs the toilet. I feel sick from the sadness and the swaying of the cart, so I have to concentrate very hard on shrinking the sickness inside me, as I have done to the tears. Nobody is talking. I try to catch the eye of Tekla, the girl sitting in front of me, but she has her arms crossed and her face is set hard in a frown. Kidlat falls asleep on my lap and I focus on being very still for him, which is easy after all my practice waiting for butterflies.

Mr. Zamora folds his insect legs up in front of him, his arms a protective cage around the glass case, and puts his white straw hat over his face. Soon he is snoring loudly and there is nothing to do but watch the passing trees.

The track we are following is well worn, but I don't know who by. I have never talked to anyone who has left our town or come from this side of the island. The forest is a thick mat of bamboo and tree ferns. Whenever Mr. Zamora snores especially loudly, it sends green birds fleeing the trees. Their calls sound like cats fighting.

The path splits and the one we take gets narrower and narrower, and soon leaves are brushing our heads. Everywhere I look, *gumamela* flowers dot the forest, and I remember Nanay's story about the house in the valley, the boy she was taken from. My *ama*. Maybe he will be sent to her now that all the Touched are coming to Culion. Maybe he and Nanay will find each other again. This is the happiest thought I've had all day.

We pass an untended grove of mangoes and the too-sweet smell makes my mouth water. The grove has obviously been abandoned a long time. The trees have grown tangled together, and the boughs hang heavy with fruit. Datu leans out as we pass and snatches one. I laugh with the others as the skin splits in his hand, but when he turns it over, the pulp is black and teeming with flies and we all stop laughing as he throws it from the cart. He sits with his dirty hand outstretched, watching it carefully as if it might try to leap onto his face.

We are almost out of the mango grove when Tekla points and screams.

"Snake! Snake!"

I spin around, heart thumping. It is only a jade vine strangling a branch, but the horses startle at her cry and send the cart swerving. I cling on as the driver pulls them to a halt and hear a crash at the front of the cart.

The glass case has smashed to shards in the dust. And beside it the two brown boxes have tipped over, their air-holed lids askew. Mr. Zamora snatches at the nearest one, but only knocks the lid clean off.

And suddenly the air is full of wings.

A patch of butterflies wafts upward, purple and yellow and green and gleaming, shimmering like a thrown scarf. My mouth hangs open, dust tickling my throat, more dust coating my tongue, as Mr. Zamora kicks the road in temper.

"Stop them!" he bellows, his thin throat ballooning like a bullfrog's. But no one is paying attention to him. All we can see is the butterflies, and all I can think of is Nanay. There are maybe two dozen of them, twisting toward the mango grove as if they are one body, or a flame, or ash from a flame. And like ash, they scatter as a long, thin hand snatches at them.

"No!" I shout as one, large-bodied and purple-winged, is knocked from its current of air, its colors suddenly snuffed out in the dark cage of Mr. Zamora's hand. The rest snap away like a tail. I try to follow their trail but it is like the stars all over again. The shadows shift and change their moorings, impossible to catch.

It is as if someone has let a clock tick again. We all slump as the butterflies disappear, and Mr. Zamora brings his hand up to his eye and squints inside. He sighs heavily and clenches it into a fist. I hear a faint, brittle sound, like the shell of a nut cracking. He takes a deep breath before he speaks, his voice low and dangerous.

"I damaged the wing," he says to no one in particular, brushing the fragmented body onto the ground. "No use to anyone."

He rounds suddenly on us. "Who was it who screamed?"

No one looks at the girl who cried "Snake." I focus on a point just beyond his left ear.

"Whoever it was, you lost me thirty of my finest specimens. If any of you make so much as a squeak from now on, I will make you walk the rest of the way."

He stares us all down for a few more moments, then bends, pulling a clean kerchief from his pocket. He uses it to carefully sift through the broken glass, and picks up three sticks, the chrysalises dangling. He rests them across his long forearms, and climbs back up beside the driver. We move on.

After a couple of hours of silence, the trees start pressing close to the cart. The driver has to stop a few times to hack at the foliage with a machete.

"Are you sure this is the right way?" says Mr. Zamora. "I was assured the path had been prepared."

The driver shrugs. "I have never come this way before. They're sending a workforce next week to broaden it."

The sun is sinking and the forest seems even more impenetrable than before. The rainy season is coming, and the trees seem to have spread themselves out very wide in readiness to catch the water.

A feeling rises, like a hook behind my navel. Mr. Zamora and the driver aren't looking. If I could somehow tell the others to be silent, then maybe I could slip away. Maybe some of them would come with me.

But then the hook loosens and all the sensible thoughts come rushing in. It would not take them long to catch me up. And even if I got back to Nanay, she would only get in trouble and I would be sent back. Nothing would change.

The driver is climbing back up and clicking his tongue, and we are pushing on through the forest.

We do not stop again until the trees thin and suddenly end. Ahead the sea is flat as a puddle, the same purple-bruised gray as the dusk sky. We have traveled a whole day away from Culion Town. Nanay will be making dinner, or else sitting on our front step with a cup of cooling tea. Perhaps Bondoc and Capuno are with her. I see her as clearly as if I were there too. I close my eyes for a moment. I must keep this picture safe.

The beach here is made of uneven stone slabs that turn to drums beneath the horses' hooves. A harbor, hastily built. It curves like a necklace laid out at the edge of the forest, jewel-bright lamps lit at unsteady intervals. Unfinished though it is, it feels far too grand to be sitting here in the middle of nowhere. Mr. Zamora must have ordered the *Sano* port to be one of the first things built. The stars are sifted through thin clouds, and the moon is just gathering strength. And sitting in the water is a boat, bigger than the one that brought the Touched.

"A ship!" says one of the boys excitedly, but it is not at all how I thought a ship would be. There are no sails, no rope ladders or masts. Just a metal column belching smoke and a gray, smooth hull, thin and pointed. It is as miserable as the reason it is here, a storm cloud offering no hope of the relief of rain.

There are men here, with closed gray faces. They shoulder Mr. Zamora's luggage and he buzzes around them, saying, "Be careful, be careful!" as they carry the boxes of butterflies into the darkness of the ship.

We wait on the cart in huddled silence until we are unloaded much like the luggage, without speaking or smiles. Mr. Zamora unfurls a piece of paper and reads out one name at a time, to check we are all here. The little boy Kidlat puts his hand up at his name and I have to answer for him.

We cross the narrow plank and Kidlat holds my hand to steady himself as the boat rocks. We are led into a low-ceilinged cabin, where we are seated on benches along the walls. Everything is metal and bolted to the floor. The smell is metallic too, and heady. It sends queasiness spreading through my stomach.

Mr. Zamora does not follow us. He walks past the cabin along the narrow deck to the front of the boat. He keeps his face pointed forward, even when the vessel begins to move, so smoothly it takes me a moment to realize we are going, actually going.

Everyone floods to press their hands against the large back window, to watch the hilly, jagged outline of Culion drop back to lie low on the horizon. Even the boys, who care so much about seeming tough, cry when we lose the necklace lights of the harbor to the dark distance of night.

"Settle down, children," says one of the men, not unkindly. "It's a couple of hours to Coron. I'd get some sleep."

Eventually the others drift away from the window and try to make themselves comfortable on the hard floor. I stay, face turned back, as if Mr. Zamora and I are two opposite points on a clock face, or compass, both pushing toward and away from something.

The Orphanage

B eing on the sea is like the minutes after spinning around as fast as you can—walking straight is difficult when your body remembers turning. Everything tilts when it shouldn't, even when you are sitting still. My neck aches and my eyes itch but I don't sleep and I don't stop looking back toward Culion even when it is only a direction somewhere across the sea. I lose track of time but it is long enough for the bruised sky to deepen into darkest blue. The moon is bright as a smile and the stars are so many and fall so often it makes my chest pang with missing Nanay.

A few times the tall shape of Mr. Zamora strides past the large window as he paces around the deck. He walks with his hands behind his back, leading with his head. He talks constantly to himself, but silently, his lips moving quickly behind the glass. *He's sick.* Capuno's words had been filled with pity, and now I feel it, briefly, as I watch the Director of Health's authorized representative walk alone and talk to no one.

When Mr. Zamora, out of sight at the front of the boat, calls, "Land ahead!" I finally face forward, rubbing my sore neck as the others stir. There are lights in the distance, much like the harbor on Culion. When we dock, there is a cart with two horses waiting, as if we have done a slow circle and come back to our start. But the horses are a different color, the driver a different man, and the harbor is backed by a town, the houses more uniform than on Culion, the roads wider. We are unloaded from the boat and reloaded onto the cart. There is no forest here, only a broad dirt street that has been well flattened and cleared of stones. Some of the houses still have lights on but shutters close sharply when we pass.

My chest is full of a heavy ache. Every step the horses take drags me farther from home and deeper into a new life. It feels nothing like an adventure.

The road curves right and we climb a steep hill, the horses straining and blowing. When the road levels, we are at a pair of wooden gates. The horses stop, snorting as the driver swings down to open them.

After the gates there are trees again, and ahead the shape of a large building spreads across the ground. A door opens at the center, and a figure steps out, backed by light. I see another muffled light twitch at the top right-hand window, but then the light disappears and I hear shutters closing. Perhaps the other children are watching us arrive. My chest tightens. I hope they will like us.

The figure turns human-sized. It is a woman, her face stern, a moon floating in her gray habit. My heart leaps, but of course it is not Sister Margaritte. This woman has bigger cheeks, and her lips are pursed, a bit like how a squirrel looks when chewing.

"Sister Teresa," says Mr. Zamora expansively as he steps stiffly from the cart. "How nice to see you again."

"Mr. Zamora." Sister Teresa nods. Already I can tell she doesn't approve of him. She scans us as we step down from the cart. I don't think she approves of any of us. My leg has gone to sleep and I have to hit it a couple of times before the blood comes tingling back. We stand in a line as if for inspection, though no one has told us to.

"You are well trained," says Sister Teresa dryly, then walks slowly along the line, asking our names.

"It's late," says Sister Teresa after we have introduced ourselves. "You must be tired." Kidlat yawns as if on cue, and she raises her eyebrows at him. "Cover your mouth next time. For now, I will show you to your beds. Tomorrow I will explain the rules. Tonight two will suffice: no talking after bedtime, and no getting out of bed in the night unless you need the privy. Understood?"

Everyone nods except me, who says, "Yes, Sister Teresa," in a singsong, like in school. A couple of the girls giggle, and the nun's eyes flash over me. I do not know if I am being praised or not.

"Boys, follow Mr. Zamora. Girls"—she motions inside and to the right—"follow me."

Mr. Zamora clears his throat. "Sister Teresa, am I to understand I will be sleeping in the dormitory?"

Sister Teresa had turned away but now she pivots back, very slowly and on her heels, so it looks as if the ground has moved rather than her. She is a bit terrifying.

"Yes," she says in a clipped tone. "That is what you are to understand."

Mr. Zamora is undeterred. "I was led to believe I would have my own quarters."

Sister Teresa's lips twitch. "So you do."

She points to a shadow to the right of the building, which resolves itself into a pile of bamboo sticks. "You're welcome to stay there if you wish."

A few of the others laugh and Mr. Zamora glares around at us. "Why is it not ready?"

"Because you were in such a rush to take these children from their families, you have arrived early. Come, girls."

But before she can lead us inside, Mr. Zamora steps in front of her. His voice is sickly sweet, but has the edge of a blade embedded in it. "Sister, let's not get off to a bad start. Do I need to remind you that the funding for this place is entirely reliant on my plans to bring the Culion children here? That the government paid to build the new story at my command?" He gestures at the orphanage behind him.

I notice that the top part of the building does look newer, its paintwork brighter, and there is glass in the windows, whereas on the lower floor there are only shutters.

"And if we cannot get along," continues Mr. Zamora, "it will not be my position in jeopardy. Do we understand each other?"

I cannot see Sister Teresa's face, but her voice comes out just as sweet and dangerous as his. "Perfectly." With this she sweeps around him and inside as if she wore a silk cloak and not a cotton habit.

I snatch a glance at Mr. Zamora before I follow with the others. His lips are pressed together so tightly they are white. He notices me looking and a hissing sound escapes his mouth. I drop my head.

The light comes from candles in the central room. Its details are picked out by the thin brightness—desks, chairs, a smudged blank blackboard. There is a door leading off each side of the room, another beside the board, and a set of narrow stairs disappearing up into darkness.

We turn right and enter our dormitory, with pallets and thin blankets for beds. Someone sniffs loudly. Sister Teresa shows each of us to a bed in the gloom, and indicates the direction of the privy. A sudden scuffling comes from above our heads and I think it is mice until Sister Teresa frowns and sets off upstairs. We hear her muffled warnings, and climb into bed quickly and quietly.

My bed is at the far end of the room. It is lumpy in all the wrong places, and smells faintly stale. There are etchings in the wall next to my head—a stick figure with long hair, and the letter "M." As the night settles, I can hear waves hitting rock, as though I'm sleeping on top of the sea. The whole night feels un-moored, the strangeness sharp and uncomfortable as thorns. It is only by pressing my fingers into my ears and humming one of Nanay's lullabies that I can begin to fall asleep.

The Orphans

Sister Teresa snores. It wakes me up early, and I lie with a tangle of knots in my stomach, listening to her. Twice in the night I reached for Nanay and found only emptiness. We are all red-eyed and reluctant when Sister Teresa strides up and down the room ringing a little bell. The room looks even sparser in the gray morning light. It is bigger than I realized, and there is a whole row of empty beds against the window-less back wall. The shutters on my side open onto the scrubby courtyard where we arrived.

Sister Teresa instructs us to change out of our travel clothes. All of us fell asleep in them and we look rumpled as rags. She collects them into a pile and gives them to Tekla.

"The first chore is laundry. We will organize a rota. There is soap in a box on my desk. You must ask permission before you use it, as we are not quite prepared for this number of children. I will get some more supplies today, but even then we use our resources sparingly, yes?"

I am uncertain how to answer after being the only one to speak last time, but Sister Teresa is looking at me expectantly, so I reply, "Yes, Sister Teresa."

"Thank you, Amihan. Girls, please follow her lead. Otherwise it sounds like I am talking to myself."

Tekla nudges one of the two Igmes and they snicker quietly. "Goody Two-Shoes," hisses Tekla. Heat rushes to my face, but Sister Teresa doesn't hear her.

"After we have made you presentable, you can meet the other children. They are anxious to make your acquaintance." I remember the whispers and the scuffling and hope she is telling the truth. "Let's get started, then. Follow me."

We do so, Tekla wrinkling her nose at the dirty clothes in her arms. The door to the boys' dormitory is closed, so Sister Teresa opens it and stands in the doorway ringing her bell until we hear them wake up.

"Change into clean clothes, then join us outside," she says. "Mr. Zamora?"

His face appears suddenly around the door. By the look of his bloodshot eyes and his yesterday clothes, it seems he hasn't slept.

"You will need to ensure the boys rise earlier in future. We can't fall too far behind the day."

Sister Teresa does not go up the stairs, so we have to wait to meet the other children. We follow the nun outside, leaving Mr. Zamora looking very much like he got out of the wrong side of bed, if he lay down at all.

The cart is still there, the driver asleep in the back. Sister Teresa leads us quietly past and I suspect she believes he deserves a rest more than Mr. Zamora does.

When the boys join us, rubbing their eyes in the early-morning light, we set off across the courtyard and down a narrow track through thick forest.

Kidlat keeps close behind me. His brown eyes are wide and frightened, fringed with lashes starfished together from crying. He has put his tunic on back to front and I crouch to turn it the right way around. He watches me closely, whimpering when I pull his thumb from his mouth so I can maneuver his arm out and back into the correct sleeve. I take his pudgy hand and we run to catch up with the others.

"This is the way to the river," Sister Teresa is explaining. "You can come here as often as you wish, so long as you never miss lessons, and tell someone where you are going."

The day is already full of a sticky, wet heat that hovers under the trees and makes their shade uncomfortable. The light dapples everybody a deep green, like lily pads. I follow behind one of the Igmes, but she seems to be interested only in being friends with the girl called Lilay. They walk close together, heads bowed and bodies turned slightly toward each other to fit down the narrow path. Nanay is the only person I ever told secrets to, and a horrible sinking feeling drags at my legs. She is my only true friend, and no one here seems interested in talking to me. Unless you count Kidlat, who doesn't talk.

I blink rapidly as we approach a wide, shallow river. It makes a splashing sound as it runs over rocks, and on the opposite bank the forest nudges right up to the edge, trailing branches and leaves along the surface. Flowers spread out here and there like fans.

"This is where you can do laundry, past this point." Sister Teresa indicates a large rock, then pulls out the box of soap from her habit. "Take it in turns to wash. We will establish a proper rota soon. Kidlat, you first."

It takes an hour for all of us to get clean and then to dry off with the rags Sister Teresa pulls from yet another pocket. I help Tekla with the laundry until it is my turn to bathe, swilling the clothes and then scrubbing them on the large rock with soap, but she still does not smile at me. I suppose this is her way of dealing with the weight in her chest.

Mine is to remember all the things I see and do, so I can write them in my letter to Nanay. So far I have the journey here—cart, boat, cart—the little bell Sister Teresa uses and her seemingly endless pockets. I hope the way Sister Teresa treats Mr. Zamora will make Nanay laugh.

There is no sign of him when we get back, but the cart driver has lit the fire pit and is cooking a large omelet. There is a small mountain of eggshells at his feet. My mouth waters as he throws in a handful of wild chives.

"This is Luko," says Sister Teresa. "I doubt he introduced himself to you—he doesn't talk much. Luko is our cook, though soon we will have more staff arriving from the mainland."

Luko turns on his haunches and nods at us. He is built like Bondoc, and has hair that grows straight up and out from his head. I add the fact that we have a cook to my mind-letter.

"I shall go and fetch the other children, and you can make your introductions over breakfast. Luko, can you fetch Tildie for me?"

Luko moves the pan off the fire and heads around the side of the building. Igme and Lilay set to whispering as Sister Teresa disappears into the shade of the orphanage. In the daylight I can see that it has two floors like Dr. Tomas's house, but it is at least six times wider and has no balconies. It is painted a muted yellow, with the newer section a richer shade, and above the door in thick black letters it says CORON ORPHANAGE. At the very top a bronze cockerel turns in the wind.

The shutters are open at the top right window, and I wonder if whoever saw us arrive last night watched us leave for the river this morning. We hear the tramping of many feet on the stairs, and Sister Teresa leads two lines of children blinking into the sunlight. They all wear worn but uncreased clothes, and their faces are clean, their hair brushed and parted perfectly. Sister Teresa stands in the middle and they separate in a straight line on either side of her, boys on one side, girls on the other. It feels as though we are about to start a game, and our Culion side would lose. Kidlat slips his hand into mine.

All of them look straight ahead, except one girl at the far end of her line. She is paler than the others, paler than any of us, her hair light and flyaway, making a halo around her head. She scans us as we scan them, and stops on me. Her eyes are huge and widely spaced. I blink and she looks away.

"Children, meet your new companions. I am going to town to collect some more supplies—as you can see, Luko has used all the eggs. Mr. Zamora?" Sister Teresa calls into the shade of the building. Mr. Zamora comes outside in clean clothes, his tie knotted tightly and his straw hat pulled low. "Can you please keep an eye on the children until I return?"

"I am nearly done setting out my samples—"

"Please." Sister Teresa's voice is careful. "Just while I'm away."

"No," snaps Mr. Zamora, a ropy vein in his neck taut. "You can wait for me to finish."

Luko returns with one of the horses that collected us from the harbor. This must be Tildie. Sister Teresa purses her lips while Mr. Zamora goes back inside. We wait in silence for several minutes. Sister Teresa's foot taps impatiently. As soon as Mr. Zamora reemerges, the cook leans down, making a cradle of his hands, and Sister Teresa swings herself up onto the horse easily. Without another word she digs her heels into Tildie and they take off at a gallop down the long drive. Watching a nun on a horse is like watching a dog walk on its hind legs: like a trick.

Mr. Zamora hovers uncertainly outside the orphanage. It

seems as if he does not want to come close to us. He drags a chair from the schoolroom and sits on the threshold, eyes flicking over us as though we could attack at any moment. I think of the samples, the live butterflies somewhere inside. Nanay would have loved watching them escape back in the forest, the twisting, colorful rope of them darting beyond Mr. Zamora's fingers.

Luko squats by the fire again, throwing in something diced that scents the air with a mouthwatering sharpness. The orphanage children are still lined up like Mr. Zamora's butterflies, neat and impenetrable. After a few more long seconds Datu steps forward and holds out his hand to the tallest boy in the line.

"I'm Datu."

The boy wrinkles his nose and brushes past Datu. The other orphans follow him to sit in a neat circle by Luko, making the logs they sit on look like thrones. They leave no spaces for us. Datu drops his hand.

"Hey," he says. "I was just introducing myself."

Silence from the orphans.

Luko raises a bushy eyebrow. "I think he's talking to you, San."

The tallest boy sniffs. "I don't want to catch it."

"Catch what?" says Luko.

"The rotting disease." San shudders. "They're from that island. They're dirty."

My stomach flips. They are not going to be kind. They speak like Mr. Zamora. I hear a creak as the man leans forward in his chair to watch.

Luko cuffs the boy lightly over the head. "They don't have it, that's why they're here."

"You can never be too careful," Mr. Zamora says, his hands plucking at his sleeves.

"Nonsense," says Luko, then checks himself as Mr. Zamora glares. "No disrespect, sir, but it's not like catching a cold."

"Anyway, we just washed," Datu says, and all of the orphans' heads turn toward him. "Sister Teresa took us to the river."

"Great," says San. "Now we can't use the river."

"Why not?" one of the other orphans asks, eyes wide.

"The rotting disease hides in the water," says San in a low voice. It is suddenly silent—even the trees stop rustling, the fire stops crackling. "It waits on the drying rocks, in the moss, waiting for unsuspecting victims to come and—" Luko gives him another clip around the ear as Mr. Zamora leans back in his chair, the corners of his mouth turned up. He's enjoying this, I realize.

"You're talking nonsense, talking ghost stories," Luko snaps, taking the pan off the fire and sharing out the eggs.

San laughs, but it is an unkind laugh. I don't think he means all of what he says, but he believes it enough for his meanness to spread over us. The other orphans laugh too, but uneasily, and turn back to the meal. All except the pale girl. She takes her bowl and brings it to our huddled group. She sets it down in front of Kidlat.

"Here," she says, and holds out a spoon. He takes it like a present.

She goes back and gets another bowl and places it in front of Datu. "Here."

The girl walks back and forth until we all have bowls. The orphans watch her in silence, not eating, and we watch her too. I wonder why she only brings one bowl at a time until I notice her right hand. It is curled and hangs limp at the wrist. I try not to stare as she puts the final bowl down in front of me, then goes back and fetches hers. She holds up a spoon and says, "Last one. We'll have to share."

"You'll catch it, Mari!" calls one of the orphan girls.

"Or they'll catch what you've got," shouts San.

"She doesn't have it," says Mari, her voice carrying between our two circles. She turns to me. Her eyes are the color of honey, a deep gold. "Do you?"

I shake my head.

"And you can't catch this." She holds up her limp hand and smiles. "So let's eat."

The First Day

Only Mari eats with us that first morning. Only she talks to us kindly, though the others daren't say anything rude when Sister Teresa returns. San is the loudest among the orphans to answer "Yes" when the nun asks, "Did you make friends?", and I notice that whenever she is looking, he smiles affably in our direction. But when her back is turned, or only Mr. Zamora is around, he takes a half step away from us.

Mr. Zamora speaks only to the orphans, and he seems to especially dislike me. When he was asking San what happened to his parents, San told him that his father had died in a fishing accident. Mr. Zamora looked straight at me and said, "Better a dead parent than a dirty one."

I waited until Mr. Zamora went inside, then approached San.

"I'm sorry about your *ama*," I said.

San looked much as I felt: like he'd been punched. He glanced at me, his eyes glazed, and walked quickly away.

We have an hour to "get to know each other," which means us staying at one end of the dirt playground, and them at the other. Mari circles around to me several times but I don't feel like talking. I am not used to someone trying to make friends: at school the others ignored me and they seem content to carry on doing that here. But Mari keeps asking me about home and I know I will cry if I talk about any of it.

I excuse myself and go inside and sit holding Nanay's basin for a while. Mari seems kind, but she is so bold and friendly when we have just met that it makes me feel even more shy. I wipe my eyes and chew the insides of my cheeks to stop the tears coming again.

I can't spend years sitting inside with no one and nothing but Nanay's basin to talk to. Nanay would tell me to try to make friends, to make an effort. I take three deep breaths and head outside.

As I pass Sister Teresa's office, which is through the door next to the blackboard, I hear voices. The door is slightly ajar, and I pause, though I shouldn't.

"When will my quarters be built?" snaps Mr. Zamora's voice.

"Soon. Is your bed not comfortable enough in the boys' dormitory?" replies the nun.

"I think you underestimate my needs. I am writing a book—"

"A process that takes up no space except in your head."

"A book on butterflies. And far from it occupying only my thoughts, I need to have space to make more samples."

"Samples?"

"And to preserve the live samples I brought with me. And for the chrysalises. They need stability and the boys keep knocking them from the windowsills when they open the shutters."

"Heaven forbid they should have fresh air."

"Need I remind you that I am the one in charge here, Sister Teresa? You would be wise not to take that tone with me. And besides, I don't know why I have to share with the Culion children. I should be moved up to the normal ones."

"The Culion children are only here because you brought them." Sister Teresa's voice is frosty.

"On the government's orders!"

"Why have you stayed? Because of orders, or because you want to help them?"

"The government has entrusted me with the care of these children and I will undertake it!" Mr. Zamora takes a calming breath. "I am the authority here, and it is time you started treating me as such."

When the nun speaks again, her voice is more measured. "You weren't meant to arrive until next month. The men who were going to build your quarters are all working on other jobs."

"I don't know how the Director of Health expected me to spend a whole month in that place."

"I'll write to town and request they begin as soon as possible," says Sister Teresa, her polite tone cracking with impatience. I hear a floorboard creak and hurry away from the door. "In the meantime you may use this room."

There are quick footsteps, but before she appears, I run outside. Mari is sitting alone, as I left her. I hesitate a moment, then settle beside her.

"Are you all right?" she asks.

Make an effort, I tell myself. "I heard Mr. Zamora and Sister Teresa arguing."

Mari's eyes light up. "Tell me." I repeat the conversation as best I can.

"He's a butterfly collector?" says Mari when I finish.

I nod. "He has some butterflies in boxes in the boys' room, and he's growing more on the windowsills."

"What does he do with them?"

"He puts them on his walls. And I suppose he'll write about them in his book."

"Why?"

"My *nanay* says it makes him feel powerful to kill things."

"He kills them?" Mari's wide eyes go wider still. "He doesn't just wait for them to die?" I shake my head and she sucks in her cheeks. "I hope he doesn't find out my name."

"Why?"

"It's Mariposa." She wrinkles her nose. "Butterfly. My *nanay* was Spanish."

She holds out her arms and lets her tongue loll out as if she's dead and pinned. "How do I look?"

I snort with laughter in spite of myself just as Sister Teresa comes out, her cheeks pink. "Children, time to start lessons. Inside, please."

Today is mathematics and I think of Nanay as the numbers add and subtract and multiply themselves in my head. It is soothing to be allowed to fill my mind with something that reminds me of her without having to talk about her. Sister Teresa says I am very good and asks if I will help one of the other girls, Suse, with her times tables. She moves Suse next to me and Suse sits rigid, not looking at me as I point to the numbers.

It is only when Mari comes to sit with us at break time and says, "You know San's lying, don't you? She doesn't have it, and it's not in the river," that I feel Suse relax.

Throughout our lessons Mr. Zamora carries boxes from the boys' dormitory to Sister Teresa's room. The nun studiously ignores him, but Mari nudges me. "Are those the butterfly boxes?"

I nod.

"Poor things," she mutters. "Shut in the dark like that."

At lunch all the orphans are wondering what is in the boxes, and Datu tells them about the butterflies that escaped in the forest on Culion. San listens openmouthed, and he and

Datu end up talking and kicking a ball around the playground together. I think San is bored with pretending to be disgusted by us, and some of the other children start asking us questions about ourselves too. By the end of the first day most of them are speaking as if it is the first day of school—cautious, but friendly. At dinner some of the boys sit with us too, though no one shares a spoon apart from Mari and me.

"Why won't he eat?" says Mari when we have scraped our bowls clean. She nods at Mr. Zamora, who is sitting in his chair next to the pile of bamboo sticks that will be his quarters. He is writing in a small leather-bound notebook, and has not touched the bowl of rice and fish Luko laid by his feet.

"He thinks he'll catch it if he eats the same food. He thinks we're Touched, even though his own doctors say we're not."

"Touched?"

"It's what we call it. The illness."

"We use that word too," says Mari. "But it means 'ill in the head, mad.'"

"I think Mr. Zamora might be a bit ill in the head," I say.

"Why?"

I explain about the petition, and the cleaning. The blood on his hands. Mari puts on her listening face, her brow furrowed.

"Poor thing," she says when I finish, just as she did about the butterflies. I follow her gaze to Mr. Zamora. He is staring into the middle distance. He looks exhausted. "Imagine thinking dirt is so bad, and going to a place you think is dirty."

"But it's not," I say hotly.

101

"That's not what we're told here," she says gently. "On Coron lots of people think like San. People are scared of what is different. My hand, for example."

She holds it up. I have been wary of looking at it since I noticed there was something wrong.

"It's all right," she says. "You can look." Her hand lolls, and I see that some of the fingers aren't formed.

"I was born with it like this," Mari continues. "And because of it, and my skin being so pale, my parents thought I was cursed. Though since then people have thought all kinds of things. Someone in town called me a leper—sorry—Touched once."

"Is that why you're being nice to me?"

She blinks at me. "I'm nice because you're nice. I could see it even on the first night. You were comforting that little boy even though you were sad yourself."

"Was it you at the top window, watching us arrive?"

Mari nods.

"I'm below you. My bed is at the bottom right."

"Have you seen my self-portrait?"

I frown, then remember the stick figure and the "M" etched into the wall. "Oh! Yes. It's . . ."

Mari laughs: a light, lovely sound. "Terrible. I did it when I first arrived. How funny that you're in my old bed. We should pass messages!"

I clap a hand to my forehead. "I said I'd write to Nanay today."

"You can do it now."

"But it won't get to the post until Luko goes to town."

"Did you say you'd post it today, or just that you'd write it?"

"Write."

"So you're not breaking your promise. Wait here."

She gets up and disappears inside. I look around. Some of the others are kicking a ball of rags around, all playing together. So much can change in a day, but here and there around the pitch I see some Culion children—the shorter Igme and Kidlat and Lilay—sitting apart and alone. I wonder if they also feel as if their heads and hearts are left behind, stuck in Culion. I feel hollowed out. Kidlat sees me looking at him and walks over. He holds out a scrappy flower, a weed of some kind, and I take it. He smiles and sits next to me.

When Mari comes back outside she sits on the other side of him. "Hello," she says. "I'm Mari."

"He doesn't speak," I say. "But his name's Kidlat."

"Nice to meet you," Mari says. Kidlat grins. "Now." She puts some paper down in front of me. "Here. Write."

"What shall I say?"

"Whatever you want."

I scrunch up my face. "I don't know where to start."

"Start with the shape of your day. Then fill it in. I won't look."

She lies down. The air is cooler now. Insects hum and I watch the game of football for a while. San and Datu are on the same team, and Luko is in goal. He barely has to move to block the ball. Mr. Zamora is frantically scribbling in the dusk.

I'll tell Nanay he's writing a book about butterflies. I'll tell her about the journey, and Kidlat and the other children, and Sister Teresa. I'll tell her about Luko and lessons, and I'll start with sharing a spoon. I'll start with Mari.

Sister Teresa orders us all to bed early, but I lie awake, listening for the sea. It must be close by, but I still have not found it. Tomorrow I will look for it, and for Culion Island, though it will only be a low shadow smudging the distance.

Tap. Tap.

I jump and spin toward the window. It sounds as if someone is outside, but I can't see anyone, no fingers pressed to the shutters. My heart thuds as I watch and see a shadow swoop against it. A bird?

Tap. Tap. Tap.

I open the shutter hesitantly. The taller Igme stirs in the bed next to me but does not wake. In front of me dangles a stick, tied to a piece of string. Looking up, I see a pale hand swinging. Mari. I release the stick and notice a piece of paper tied around it.

Sleep well, it says. I look up again but the string is gone, the shutters are closing. I trace the "M" in the wall. *Sleep well,* I mouth. And I do.

The Letter

The next day, while everyone plays during morning break, I slip away and skirt the back of the orphanage. An overgrown path stretches through a burst of trees. I follow it through the dappled shadows until they thin and stop, like soldiers coming to a sudden halt. I'm standing at the edge of a cliff. And there, glittering and infinite, is the sea.

I squint and realize it is not quite infinite. That unmoving mark on the horizon must be Culion. My chest clenches around something sharp. Somewhere on that tiny shape is Nanay. A hand comes to rest on my back.

Mari is there, her golden eyes wide with worry. "It's all right, Ami."

She goes to hug me but I don't want to be held. Instead we shuffle forward and sit side by side, legs dangling.

After a long silence, Mari speaks.

"I'm sorry I followed you. I was actually going to show you this place today. It's my favorite part of living here. I call it Takipsilim Cliff."

"Twilight Cliff?"

She nods. "The sun sets on this side of the island, so in the evenings we could come and watch the world get colored out."

"Colored out?"

"My *ama* used to call morning the time when the world got colored in, so it makes sense that night is when it gets colored out." She smiles at me, then points across the water. "That's Culion, where you're from."

It isn't a question, but I nod anyway.

"Siddy is pointing away from it."

"Siddy?"

"The bronze cockerel on the roof. I checked before I followed you."

"The weather vane?" I raise my eyebrows. "You call it Siddy?"

"He was my first friend here," she says seriously. "When they built the top floor, they tried to get rid of him, but Sister Teresa made them keep him. The sound of him turning used to put me to sleep."

She holds her serious face just long enough for me to worry I've upset her, then pokes me in the ribs. "I'm joking. You're my first friend here." I flush at that. "He looks like a Siddy, don't you think? And if he's pointing toward the front of the orphanage, that means the wind is blowing in the direction of Culion."

"So?"

"So, if you want to send your *nanay* a message, now's a good time."

I frown at her. "How?"

"Whisper it to the wind. It'll listen to you."

"Why?"

"Your name—you and the wind, you're family." She raises her eyebrows and grins at me, but she's not making fun. "Try it. It might make you feel better."

It feels silly, but I suppose it's no different from praying. *I'm thinking of you, Nanay. Are you thinking of me?* The wind does not whisper back.

As I open my eyes, I notice a red smudge far below us in the water, like a clump of algae. "What's that?" I point.

"It's a boat. Well, it was. See that path?" She indicates a faint scribble on the side of the cliff. "I went down once. The boat was more afloat then, but barely. It's damaged. Abandoned. Like me."

"You were left here?" I ask.

Mari nods. "Sister Teresa was ordered to send me to a work-house in Manila. Because I wasn't an orphan, only not wanted."

"That's horrible," I say.

"But she didn't." Mari shrugs. "She ignored the government's orders."

I think of Dr. Tomas and Father Fernan. If they had ignored Mr. Zamora and the government's orders, I would be with Nanay right now. A hot spike of anger lances through me.

"I can't believe they left you."

"They also loved me, I think. They taught me things, about trees, and fishing, and boats. Boats most of all. My father sailed, and I remember him teaching me one-handed knots, and how to hoist the canvas to catch the wind." She smiles dreamily. "His face was so brown from the sun it was like leather."

"Then why did they—" I don't want to say the word "abandon." "Why did you end up here?"

The smile fades. "When I was seven, a witch doctor came to our village and said I was cursed, and that's why I was so pale. They said I was the reason for bad harvests, for women in the village losing their babies . . ." She trails off. "For every bad thing."

"That's not fair!"

"At least they gave me to the orphanage instead of leaving me in the forest. That's what some people do to cursed children."

"But you're not cursed."

"You're the first person who's made me feel normal. Or at least, that you're as strange as me."

"Strange?"

She fixes me with her honey eyes. "The others don't talk to us, do they? Apart from Kidlat, they don't come near us. It's as if they don't see us. But you see me, don't you? And I see you."

108

I look away, feeling a flush of embarrassment creep up my neck. "We should get back."

Mr. Zamora spends much of his time holed up in Sister Teresa's office. Though he is meant to be director of the whole orphanage and everyone in it, including Sister Teresa, he leaves her to run things day to day and only occasionally comes out to loom over us all. It is strange to see her nervous around him, when she is so fierce otherwise. Sometimes, when it is noisy after dark in the boys' dormitory, Sister Teresa only has to go and stand in the doorway and swish her habit a bit for them to fall quiet.

She sleeps and snores in the schoolroom now, though the men who are building Mr. Zamora's hut will arrive soon, so she will not have to for much longer. Nanay's letters have not arrived either. It is not like Nanay to break a promise.

Mari says she is sure Nanay has her reasons. She doesn't know anything about Nanay or her reasons, but she is only trying to be kind, so I try not to show it annoys me. Mari is still the only one who talks to me here. I would be lonely without her.

Still, I don't tell her everything I'm feeling. I keep that inside me, or whisper it to Nanay on the wind, which feels less and less silly. Nanay's metal basin is now a home for my clothes. The bottom is a bit oily, and when I wear the tunic, it smells slightly of garlic, but I like it.

I keep taking paper from the schoolroom to write letters,

and give them to Luko to take to town to post. At the bottom of each, instead of my name and kisses, I write: *One step less!*

After two weeks I wake to tapping. There is no note on the string, only a stick dancing frantically at the shutters. I open them and look up. Mari is leaning out of the window.

What? I mouth.

Look! she mouths back, pointing. I can't see anything for a long time but then suddenly there is a cart coming through the trees. Five men jump out of the back. They carry wood and tools, and one has a bundle of papers under his arm. Letters.

Mari points down to say she is coming. I dress and creep past the sleeping girls. Sister Teresa is already up and standing in the doorway, holding the letters.

"Anything for me, Sister?" I ask, trying to sound relaxed, though my heart twists and leaps and gulps. Mari clatters down the stairs, and Sister Teresa turns to us.

"Morning, Mari. Morning, Ami. You're in luck." She holds it out, a slim fold of paper. My fingertips just brush it before it is knocked to the floor.

"What's this?" Mr. Zamora snarls. He has thrown open the office door and is panting, his shirt showing sweat patches under the arms.

Sister Teresa gapes at him. "That is a letter, and it is not yours."

"For her?" He jerks his head at me. "From the colony?"

"From her mother, yes," says Sister Teresa, bending to pick it up. Mr. Zamora puts his foot on it so she cannot lift it without ripping it.

"Her mother is a leper. She has it badly, has no nose. I've seen her." He shudders and I shudder too, but with anger.

"I am aware that all the children's parents are Touched, Mr. Zamora. Now remove your boot."

"We can't allow this!" he shouts. Other children are gathering now, behind Mari on the stairs and in the doorways to the boys' and girls' dormitories, but Mr. Zamora does not seem to see anyone. "We must keep this area clean!"

"The letters are not lepers, Mr. Zamora." Sister Teresa's nose is flaring. "I understand the government has deemed it necessary to take the children from their families, but not to remove all contact. Now, the builders have arrived. I suggest you see to them."

She is shaking but her voice holds firm. Mr. Zamora grinds his heel into the letter, tearing it a little, but eventually he lifts his foot.

"We will see about these letters." He goes outside.

Sister Teresa retrieves Nanay's letter, rumpled and boot-printed. "I am sorry about that, Ami."

She hands out letters to some of the other children too, and Mari and I leave the orphanage. Mr. Zamora is talking to the men, and he glares at me as we pass.

We wait until he is not looking, then hurry to Takipsilim Cliff. I take a deep breath and open the letter.

My dearest Ami,

My hand is bad, so Sister Margaritte is typing this on her typewriter while I talk. I am sorry that this has taken so long. I have fallen behind on our letters already.

There are more and more people arriving every day. You can't imagine how busy the town is, and how confusing all the new *Sano* and *Leproso* rules are.

The hospital is very full and people aren't very happy. Now Mr. Zamora has left, there is someone else in charge called Mr. Alonso. He is not much better, but at least he isn't so fearfully skinny.

I have made some new friends, though. My neighbor is a nice girl called Lerma. She reminds me of me, because she was taken from her family and is only twenty. She is from Mindoro Island, which is where your *ama* was from.

Bondoc and Capuno are doing all right. I see Capuno most days and Bondoc came today. It took him two days to get permission and he wasn't allowed to touch us. I am not sure how we will live like this but we will try. Hopefully when you come back, they will have realized how silly they are being.

Apart from my hand and a small cold, I am in

good health. They keep us busy with helping the arrivals, and soon the hospital is to be run only by Touched, apart from the nuns and Dr. Tomas. I am going to try to get a job there so I can send you some money.

I have some bad news, but you would want to know. Rosita passed away. I hope this doesn't make you too sad. Her suffering is over, and it was time for her. Her funeral was yesterday. It was in the church, unfortunately, but it was still a very lovely send-off. I have apologized to Sister Margaritte for that remark but won't let her cross it out.

Tell me everything. I hope it is beautiful and that you are well looked after. I will write again when Sister Margaritte can type for me. She is very busy at the moment, so I can't write every day like I promised. Know that I want to.

I love you.

Nanay

"Well?" says Mari eventually. "Is everything all right?"

My skin prickles hot, the letter's words burned behind my lids, like I've stared at the sun too long. This is not how I thought I'd feel after Nanay's first letter. I thought it would be something warm and comforting, like a smooth river stone perfect to cup in a palm. This feeling is jagged and sharp. My whole body seems to shake with the strength of my heartbeat as I try to grasp the facts.

"Our friend Rosita. She died."

"Oh, no, I'm so sorry."

"She was very sick. Nanay says it was better this way."

"And your *nanay*? Is she well?"

I stare down at the letter. "She has a cold."

"That's all right, isn't it? As long as she beats it before the rainy season?"

I take a deep breath. "Yes, I suppose so. Only . . . only a complication like that—it's what Rosita had. When you're Touched, it's not the leprosy that kills you most of the time."

It's complications. Dr. Tomas explained this to us at school the day he arrived from the mainland, the only volunteer to take up a post on the island of no return. I was six years old. "Being Touched makes your body less able to fight colds and sweats and other illnesses," he said. He did not have the worry lines then that he has now. We were still textbook cases to him, not families. "You must take proper precautions. Complications like colds are what can make you very sick."

"I'm sure she will be better soon," says Mari.

"Yes." I steady my breathing. She is right. Nanay has made friends and Sister Margaritte is helping her write to me. She is all right, though the changes sound like a nuisance. I wonder what Mr. Alonso looks like. Because Nanay has said he is not skinny, I picture him as fat. It is funny how my mind thinks in opposites. Like when she says Culion has gone from Mr. Zamora

114

to Mr. Alonso, I think of Z to A. A backward alphabet. And I have gone from living in a place with sunrise to a place of sunset.

Mari is so quiet next to me I can almost forget she's there. I like this about her, that she knows when not to talk. She is looking out over the sea, escaped wisps of her pale hair blowing around her shoulders. She is the strangest and most beautiful thing I have ever seen.

The Hatching

It only takes the builders four days to construct Mr. Zamora's hut. Once they install a bolt on the door, he moves in straightaway. He spends his days and nights in the hut. Sometimes we hear hammering inside and I think he must be hanging his butterfly collection. He orders the men back to build him a separate workshop, which has such precise specifications I hear one of the builders complaining it will take them three times as long.

Mari and I spend all our time together. We play hopscotch and hide-and-seek, and sit next to each other in class. The boys are very loud, so Kidlat comes to play with us a lot. He has stopped crying so much and even laughs sometimes. I mentioned him in my letter to Nanay, so hopefully she can tell his parents I am looking after him.

Soon after Mr. Zamora moves into his hut, a quiet, cat-eyed woman called Mayumi arrives to help Sister Teresa with the housework, but Mayumi spends less time cleaning and more time helping Luko with cooking. She also stays with him in his little hut, which makes the nun suck her teeth.

Mr. Zamora only emerges from his hut to walk down to town. He does this every day, at ten in the morning. He is back just after morning lessons end—we hear him whistling tunelessly, and he goes into his hut with a box under his arm.

"Food, perhaps?" Mari wonders, but I don't think it can be, because, if anything, he seems even thinner and I saw him arguing with Luko about Mayumi only yesterday.

"Do you let her near the food?"

"Of course," said Luko, already bored with the conversation. "She helps me make it."

"But you don't know where she's been! She doesn't have papers!"

"She doesn't need them. She's from Bagac. There are no lepers there."

"I can't eat the food if she's near it."

"Then don't," said Luko, and closed the hut door in his face. Mr. Zamora kicked the door once, then spun around. I looked away a moment too late.

"You," he hissed, cheeks flushing. "You stay away from me."

He hurried back to his hut, taking a wide circle around me, even though I was nowhere near.

He also made us boil any clothes that came from Culion. My blue church dress lost all its dye. I can tell he wants to boil us, too, just to be safe. When we go down to the river, he is often there, washing his hands upstream.

"He shouldn't be around children," said Luko to Sister Teresa one morning, watching Mr. Zamora trudge toward the river for the third time in half an hour. But Sister Teresa seems powerless to stop him because he is the government's authorized representative. She told Luko that Mr. Zamora's brother is someone high up in government, in Manila, and that's why no one will get rid of him.

It is fifteen steps less and we are all outside on our lunch break when I finally see inside Mr. Zamora's hut for the first time. Mari and I are playing her one-handed version of cat's cradle when a loud shout, more urgent than the usual playground cries, makes me lose my grip and tangle the string.

Everyone turns toward the noise. The door of Mr. Zamora's hut has flown open and he is leaning out of the window, latching the shutters back. Then he disappears from sight again. Mari scrambles to her feet and I follow. The boys crowd around the open door and Mari and I drag logs to the window, stand on them and peer in.

Mari gasps, and though I have seen the pinned butterflies

before, it still takes my breath away to see them rippling across the walls. Mr. Zamora is hunched over his desk, magnifying glass in hand, one of the horizontal sticks suspended between two upright supports. One of the chrysalises is swinging wildly, looking more than ever like a dry leaf about to fall.

"Move out of the way!" he snaps at the boys at the door. "I opened that to get more light, not for you to spy."

The boys move and some of them gather around us at the window. They try to nudge us off our vantage point but we hold firm. Mr. Zamora's bloodshot eyes flick between the chrysalis and a pad of paper. He sketches furiously. His fingernails are long and scratch on the pad, sending chills up my back.

Suddenly the swinging chrysalis seems to pulse, and I notice for the first time that there is a flash of color beneath the brown—a streaked, flashing orange. The pulsing continues until a split opens at the base, and two thin black fronds poke out. Mari reaches for my hand.

The whole chrysalis cracks open, hinged near the top like a pistachio, and the orange and black of the butterfly's wings are deeper and richer than any colors I have ever seen. Even the older boys gasp, and they don't let anyone see they are interested in anything normally. The black fronds wave and scrabble, and I realize they are its feet. The butterfly is pulling itself out, flexing its wings to loosen the case and its feet to drag itself out of the crack. Suddenly it slides free, its feet gripping the chrysalis, which does not look brown or any color anymore—

just an empty papery shell, like the dried skin you pull off a scar after burning your hand.

The butterfly's wings are crimped from the cramped space within its case. Mr. Zamora is still staring and sketching, staring and sketching, using sheet after sheet of paper. The butterfly climbs up the chrysalis as if it is the farthest distance in the world, twitching its wings slightly open and closed like the heartbeats of a tiny animal. Finally it reaches the horizontal stick, and stops there, letting the breaths of its wings deepen. We are all waiting for it to fly, but it doesn't. It just sits there, growing into the world. My throat closes and I have to blink back tears. I want Nanay to be here, to see it with me.

"Make it fly, mister!" says San.

Mr. Zamora jumps, as though he'd forgotten we were there. "It won't fly, not for a while. Its wings have to open fully."

"That was beautiful," breathes Mari.

"I did not invite any of you to see," says Mr. Zamora, though he seems pleased that we all look so amazed.

"What's that thing?" San points at the discarded shape on the branch.

"A chry—" I begin, but Mr. Zamora shushes me.

"He asked *me*, girl." He turns to San and says self-importantly, "A chrysalis. It is strange you are so ignorant of these matters."

"We do not have butterfly lessons," says Sister Teresa, making all of us jump. No one noticed her entering the hut and standing in the shadows by the door. She steps forward now. "We focus on mathematics, other sciences."

"They would not be *butterfly lessons*," hisses Mr. Zamora. "The term is 'lepidoptery.' And it is a recognized science, Sister. Besides, I thought nuns didn't believe in the sciences."

"Of course we do," snaps Sister Teresa. "We just believe that God is at the root of all things."

"Science is the root." Mr. Zamora's nostrils flare. "And I'm quite tired of you filling the children's heads with information to the contrary. I believe I will undertake some of their education myself. I could teach them lepidoptery, and thus natural history, natural selection."

"That is not in your purview!" Sister Teresa takes a deep breath and steadies her voice. "We do not have the equipment for such lessons."

"I will apply to the government for funds," says Mr. Zamora, scenting victory. "It is decided." He turns to the windows. "Now go away, I have work to do."

We climb down and the shutters bang closed. I feel bad for Sister Teresa, but still a kernel of excitement sits under my ribs.

"Do you think she'll let him teach us about butterflies?" I whisper.

"I don't think she has much choice," says Mari.

Butterfly Lessons

Mari is right. The following Monday Sister Teresa announces in a disapproving voice that we will begin to have lepidoptery classes once a week. Mr. Zamora comes to our first class clutching a sheaf of papers under one arm. It is like how he entered church all those weeks ago, except the sharpness of his gestures is exaggerated by how much weight he has lost. There are dark hollows under his eyes, shadows where once there was flesh. His shirt hangs loosely, a large gap between his collar and his Adam's apple. He has tied string around the waist of his trousers to keep them up.

He clears his throat. Some of the boys at the back won't stop talking. San and Datu and the other older boys have forgotten how mesmerized they were by the hatching and have gone back to acting like they don't care about anything. When Sister Teresa announced the classes, they all rolled their eyes and Datu said, "Butterflies are for *girls*," though when Sister Teresa asked him why he thought so, he only spluttered and shrugged.

Mr. Zamora claps his hands twice, but they still don't stop. He holds up a hand and rakes his long fingernails across the board with a teeth-chattering screech. We hold our hands over our ears, and he smiles.

"When I am ready to begin, you must be ready to begin. Anyone who does not behave will be punished. Understood?"

The boys mutter.

"Good." Mr. Zamora starts to line up his papers on the desk. He does this very, very slowly, and again I am taken back to Culion, with him lining up his magnifying glass and tweezers.

"So, lepidoptery." Mr. Zamora writes it on the blackboard, pressing too hard with the chalk. "I once met a stupid man who thought it was 'leper-doptery'—"

I bristle. He's talking about Bondoc, in Dr. Tomas's house.

"But in fact, the words have the same root. 'Leprosy' comes from *lepido,* meaning 'scaly.' " He grimaces. "Having encountered such people myself, I can attest to the suitability of the word. It is quite disgusting to behold."

My face flushes with anger and a chair scrapes near the back. I turn to see Datu on his feet, his face thunderous. He is thinking of his father, I'm sure, just as I am thinking of Nanay. "How dare—" the boy begins, but Mr. Zamora looks up sharply, and smiles at Datu. It is as scary as a shout.

123

"I think you had better sit down, boy."

After a moment's hesitation, Datu does so. The class lets out a collective sigh of relief.

"And Lepidoptera, the word for the order of butterflies and moths," continues Mr. Zamora, switching back to his official, class-teaching voice, "means 'scaled wing.' Butterfly wings are actually made up of many overlapping scales—though I'm sure you will agree the effect is far more pleasing on wings than it is on faces."

Datu makes another angry sound, stifled just too late.

"Come to the front, boy," says Mr. Zamora in a low voice. He still doesn't address any of us Culion children by name. Datu slouches up to him. Mr. Zamora takes Sister Teresa's wooden ruler from beside the blackboard, and the nun starts up from her seat at the back.

"I will not allow you to strike this child."

"I was not going to." Mr. Zamora nudges Datu's arms up with the ruler until they are outstretched as if on a cross, then marks the wall beneath each arm with chalk. "You will stay with your arms up like that for the full duration of this lesson. If they drop below the line, you will be struck."

"Is this really necessary, Narciso?" Sister Teresa sounds bewildered.

Mari nudges me. *Narciso!* she mouths. It would be funny normally, but his bizarre behavior is making my stomach twist.

"Discipline is necessary, yes."

Mr. Zamora rests his knuckles on the desk. He takes a deep

breath, then fixes his bloodshot eyes on each of us in turn, and begins to speak.

"Our first lesson is on the large tortoiseshell, the butterfly you saw hatch. This butterfly frequents European countries. I had my samples sent from London. I like to breed them from egg stage—something only a very experienced lepidopterist can attempt. They usually prefer to pupate in elm, and again, it takes an expert to achieve what I did."

Once he finds his rhythm, it is impossible not to listen to him. His voice grows and strengthens like the butterfly's wings, and he soon takes to pacing up and down as he did in church. Behind him, Datu's forehead shines, and his arms begin to shake after only a few minutes. Every time they start to dip below the line, Mr. Zamora hits the wall just below them with the ruler.

I am stuck somewhere between disgust and fascination. I feel horrible for Datu, but Mr. Zamora is transfixing, speaking without notes in his low voice. I sneak a look at the boys at the back and even they are listening intently. At one point Mr. Zamora explains how the caterpillar becomes liquid inside the chrysalis before forming its butterfly shape, and San whistles. Mr. Zamora holds out the empty chrysalis and points out how it has lost all its color, but that once it was a shade of rusty bronze. He holds up a colored sketch to show us. It is amazingly detailed, with shading underneath so it almost looks as if I could reach out and pluck it from the paper. Kidlat stretches his pudgy fingers out to it, but Mr. Zamora jerks it away.

"It even has metallic spots on the dorsal side, very charac-teristic."

Sister Teresa clears her throat. "Mr. Zamora, time's up."

Behind him, Datu collapses, hugging his arms to himself. Sister Teresa hurries to him, but Mr. Zamora simply gathers up his papers, and steps around the boy and the nun crouching beside him.

The smell of Luko and Mayumi's cooking wafts through the open door and we head for the eating circle. Mari and I are the last to leave the schoolroom, and as we step into the brightness, we see Mr. Zamora disappearing into the shadows of his hut. He looks triumphant.

The next lessons pick up where he left off. Occasionally he re-members something that makes him flap his hands in excite-ment and rifle through his sketches to talk about a particular detail. Four weeks into butterfly lessons he has more samples to show us, but we are still only at the chrysalis stage. We are all very well behaved—the memory of Datu wincing at the wall makes sure of that—though once the shorter Igme had a coughing fit and Mr. Zamora roared at her to get out. His tem-per sits below the surface like a second skin, fanged and quick as a snake. He still eats only fruit picked from the trees, and his hands are still raw, scoured and scarred red. When he paces, he gives off a smell of antiseptic.

I still send thoughts from the twilight cliff to Culion most days, and I empty Nanay's basin of my clothes to put it under my pillow. It isn't very comfortable but it makes me think of her.

She still has not written another letter. I am beginning to wonder if she needs to put something like a basin under her pillow to remind her of me.

"I think she's forgotten me," I say to Mari as we look out over the cliff. It is still our secret—we always make sure no one follows us.

"Impossible," says Mari. "It's just that it's harder being left than leaving. She's probably trying to get on with things."

I listen to her words, but they don't sink in. I have a feeling pressing into my skin, uncomfortable as a rash—an uneasiness. I end every thought with *One step less!* And also *Are you all right, Nanay?*

The Killing Jar

M r. Zamora is in full flow. We have finally reached the "emergence" stage, which is what we saw happen in his office.

"Once it has emerged, it takes some hours for the wings to be hard and strong enough for flight. You remember how it flapped them lightly? That was so they'd dry quicker."

Mr. Zamora reaches down and carefully places a cloth-covered dome on the desk. With a flourish he removes the cloth. Mari leans forward to see better, and so do many of the other children. I can just make out a glass jar with what looks like a slice of mango at the bottom. The large tortoiseshell swoops and dives as though it is drunk, hitting the sides of the glass.

The children ooh and aah, but all I can think is how horrible it must be to be trapped in there.

"The final stage for this butterfly is preservation," says Mr. Zamora. "Now that we are done with our demonstration, I can process the butterfly. Do you have a question?"

I turn around. San has his hand up. Mr. Zamora only acknowledges questions from the orphans. "What does 'process' mean?"

"It means this." Mr. Zamora holds up a clear bottle and a gauze pad. "Chloroform."

He places a cloth over his mouth, and tips some liquid onto the gauze. I get a noseful of something chemical. It makes my head spin. Then he lifts the dome slightly and slides the gauze inside. Somewhere at the back of my woozy mind, I know I am not going to like what happens next. The butterfly continues to swoop, but soon its movements become more purposeful. It throws itself against the glass with an almost sickening rhythm.

"Stop!" shouts Mari. "You're hurting it." Kidlat starts to cry.

"It'll be over soon," says Mr. Zamora. His gaze is fixed on the dying butterfly, and all my fear of him returns. He is enjoying watching it die. Mari is up on her feet and running to the front. She goes to lift the jar but Mr. Zamora holds her wrist.

"Don't you dare!" he cries, but Mari lifts her crumpled right hand and knocks the jar over. It smashes to the floor.

But it is too late, we can all see it. The butterfly has fallen on the gauze, its wings stilled.

"Idiot child," hisses Mr. Zamora. "You broke my killing jar!"

He is still gripping Mari's wrist and I can see her skin going white from the pressure. He raises his hand and I can see that it is not going to be a light cuff.

"Mr. Zamora!" Sister Teresa hurries to the front. "Control yourself."

But Mr. Zamora's hand is not stayed by Sister Teresa's words. He has caught sight of Mari's right hand. "Leper," he croaks, releasing her at once. "Leper!"

"She is not," says Sister Teresa, drawing Mari close beside her. "She has had it from birth."

"She is deformed?" says Mr. Zamora, eyes fixed on Mari's hand with a sickening interest. "What caused this?"

Mari puts her hand behind her, and starts to back away.

"Stay where you are," he says. "You broke my killing jar. You will fix it."

We all look down at the shards on the floor. It is cracked into many pieces.

"Mr. Zamora, it is impossible—" starts Sister Teresa.

"She will try." Mr. Zamora's eyes glint meanly. "Or else."

"Or else what?" Sister Teresa is flushed, her voice sharp.

"This is the girl you wrote to the government about, no? The one who was abandoned."

There is a pin-drop silence. I want to stop him talking, to drag Mari outside, but I feel paralyzed.

"I should have realized earlier. How many children are born so freakish?" Mari flinches. "I was there when the letter came in about the white girl. You were ordered to put her into a work-house, I believe?"

Sister Teresa is trembling, but Mari is quite still. She is watching Mr. Zamora as though he were a nest full of wasps.

"I remember now," says Mr. Zamora, enjoying our rapt attention. "And I'm sure my brother would be most interested to learn what became of her, and how the nun flouted a direct order and spent valuable funds, put aside for orphans, on a girl who should be earning her keep."

"Please, Mr. Zamora." Sister Teresa's voice shakes as much as her hand. "I—"

"So really it is the least the child can do," he interrupts. "To fix my killing jar?"

"Yes, sir," Mari says clearly.

"It is settled, then." Mr. Zamora collects his papers. "You can bring the pieces to my workshop. I have materials there you can use."

He leaves a stunned silence in his wake, like the hush just before the monsoon falls like a sheet, as if the world is holding its breath. Mari kneels and begins to sweep the pieces onto a sheet of paper. Sister Teresa looks as though she has been slapped.

"Dinner, children," she manages, then crosses to her office and closes the door. Everyone rushes to leave but I go to help Mari, holding the paper steady while she collects the glass.

"Are you all right?" It is a stupid question, and she doesn't answer me. "He can't make you fix this."

131

"He can," says Mari simply.

"But how? Even if there were fewer pieces, surely with your hand—"

Her glare cuts me short. "You don't think I can do it?"

Before I can say any more, she folds the paper up and carries the glass outside. My body feels heavy, and I stay sitting a moment. The dead butterfly is still on the gauze. I sweep it carefully into my palm, but my hand is damp and the wings powder and stick. I brush it into the wastepaper basket, the crumpled wings shining forlornly until I bury it deeper beneath used mathematics sheets.

When I go out into the courtyard, Mari is not there. Mr. Zamora is sitting on a chair outside the closed door of his workshop.

"She's inside," says Luko, coming over to me. "He says she can't come out until it's fixed. Sister Teresa should send word to Manila."

But if Sister Teresa does that, Mari will be sent to the workhouse.

Luko places a reassuring hand on my shoulder. "He'll calm down soon, I'm sure."

The cook pads back to the fire. Mr. Zamora already looks very calm to me. He is smiling that dead-eyed smile of his. Kidlat moves toward me, holding two bowls of noodles, and together we sit on the scrubby ground beside the orphanage door, and watch the workshop.

*   *   *

The stars are pricking through a dark sky before Mr. Zamora unfolds himself from the chair and opens the workshop door. He enters and after a moment Mari comes out. She is even paler than usual, her head bowed. I hurry to stand, legs numb and full of tingles, reaching her as Mr. Zamora closes the door behind her.

"Are you all right?" I say. She stumbles slightly. "What happened?"

It makes no sense for her to be so weak—she has been in there a couple of hours at most.

"Just a bit dizzy," she says. The other children begin to crowd around, and she bows her head even lower. "Can we go to the cliff?"

I wrap my arm around her waist and mumble something to the others about her feeling a bit sick so they back off. I shake my head at Kidlat when he tries to follow, and he sticks his thumb in his mouth.

We walk slowly to the cliff, and when we get there, Mari flops down on the ground. She takes in three deep breaths.

"Oh, that's so much better!"

"What happened? Why were you dizzy?"

Mari rolls onto her side. "That room, it has no windows, and he keeps all his chemicals in there. My head feels all sloshy."

I remember the whiff of chloroform, how it made my head spin. "How awful."

"It stank. As for the jar, it's impossible—though you guessed that already, didn't you?"

"I shouldn't have said that. I'm sorry—" I start to apologize, but she is grinning.

"It's all right. It just annoys me when people think I can't do something because of my hand."

A huge wave of relief crashes through me at her words, washing away the worry stuck in my throat. "Did you manage to fix some of it?"

Mari snorts. "Not in the slightest. He says I have to try again tomorrow, but I'll never be able to do it. No one could. I expect he'll get bored with waiting and buy one sooner rather than later. Won't want to be without his *killing jar* long." She shudders at the words.

I want to ask her if she is worried about his threat to send her to the workhouse, but she is back to her normal self and I don't want to bring it up. We sit listening to the lull and wash of the sea until Sister Teresa's bedtime bell calls us back.

The Burning

After lunch, Mari is ushered back to the workshop. I cram my orange into her pocket before she stands up, and Kidlat does the same. A mouthed *Thank you* and then she is gone for the afternoon. I am distracted all through mathematics, even answering Sister Teresa's question wrong, though it is a sum so basic even Kidlat could get it right.

That evening he and I assume our watching position again, and as soon as Mr. Zamora unlatches the door, I hurry to Mari. Her eyes are bright with excitement, and she is holding her arm strangely around her stomach, as though hurt.

"What's wrong with your—"

But Mari grabs my hand. "Quickly."

I feel small fingers, sticky with orange juice, wrap around my other hand but I shake them off.

"No, Kidlat," I snap. "Stay here." He watches solemnly while we disappear out of sight, and I push down the prickle of guilt as Mari drags me in her unsteady wake. An afternoon spent inhaling chemicals has muddied her balance but still she pulls me along, almost running to the cliff. She spins around at the edge to face me, her golden eyes blazing.

"Ami, I found the letters."

My heart takes a fluttering, hummingbird beat. "What do you mean?"

She draws an envelope from her pocket. My name is on the front.

"What?" My head feels light, as if I have been the one breathing chemicals. "How did you get this?"

"Stole it, obviously! Come on, Ami," says Mari impatiently. "Take it."

The envelope smells of chloroform, and of oranges from the peel in Mari's pocket. Nanay's message is inside, but what if it is bad news? I can't bring myself to open it. I slip it into my pocket.

"Aren't you going to read it?"

"Where was it?"

"You know those boxes we see him coming back from town with? Well, I opened some and found a whole pile of letters, a stack high as here." She gestures to her knee. "Look."

She moves her hand from her stomach, and tens of envelopes pour from her tunic, pooling around her ankles. She reaches into her other pocket and pulls out more letters. I catch sight of one addressed to Datu, another to one of the Igmes. I blink at her. What she's telling me isn't making sense.

"Don't you understand?" She shakes the fan of letters at me. "He's been intercepting letters from Culion. We have to tell Sister Teresa," I hear Mari say through the pulse in my ears. "He can't get away with this."

"I beg your pardon."

Mari freezes, and the voice sends a splinter of ice through my chest. We turn. Mr. Zamora is standing in the mouth of the dark forest, the torch burning in his hand turning his gaunt face into a maze of shadows.

"I was wondering where you kept sneaking off to. And aren't I glad I followed, or else I wouldn't know you were a nasty little sneak thief." He advances on Mari, who is still clutching her sheaf of letters.

"You're the sneak thief," she says boldly. "You've been stealing the letters from Culion."

"I am in charge here," he hisses. "And I decide what communication gets through. Those letters are contaminated—"

"They are not!" shouts Mari. "That's not how it works—"

"I am the scientist here!" His eyes bulge. "I was sending those letters for testing in Manila, to prove that they are dirty, dangerous—" He breaks off and breathes heavily. "But you have broken the box's seal. You've ruined everything—"

He raises his hand as if to strike her, and the blood rushes to my head. I step between them, heart pounding, and Mr. Zamora reels back as if from a snake.

"You stay away." He waves the torch at me. He still thinks I'm Touched, like Nanay. And that means he's scared of me. My own fear burns down into something sharp. I take another step toward him and he stumbles slightly, calling over my head to Mari, "You bring those letters back to my workshop immediately."

"You want to take them now?" Mari throws some at him and they flutter like gulls. One lands on Mr. Zamora's foot and he scuffs it away. He doesn't want to touch them with his bare hands.

But what he does instead is far worse. He looks from me to the letter, and back again. Then, a thin smile stretching his thin cheeks, he touches the torch to it.

It goes up instantly, a sudden flare of brightness against the grass. Anger bristles through me. Whose letter was that? Igme's? Kidlat's? Another from Nanay?

"You can't do that," Mari says indignantly, but Mr. Zamora is beyond listening, beyond hearing us. He looks around for more letters, and brings the torch down again and again, even as Mari and I rush to rescue the scattered envelopes. Mr. Zamora sets each one blazing, ignoring our cries for him to stop. They flare like beacons, or fallen stars.

The man advances on the larger pile, and though Mari is standing, trying to scoop the letters into her pockets, he sets them alight too. She yelps and jumps away, and together we shove at him, trying to knock the torch from his hand. Laughing wildly, he dodges away and begins to back toward the cliff edge, swooshing the torch through the air in front of him. The heat comes horribly close to my cheek, a blistering kiss of pain as the tip of flame brushes by.

"Stop!" Mari shouts, pulling me back toward the trees. I am furious, fighting her. I want to pull the torch from his hands, shove him over the cliff, anything to stop him laughing. Heat is pulsing through my whole body, down the backs of my legs, across my shoulders.

"Ami, stop!"

Wheeling around on Mari, ready to push her if she won't let me go, I finally realize what she is pulling me from. It is not anger making my skin burn hot—it is fire. Around the burned letters the grass, dead and dry and waiting for the monsoon, has caught like tinder. What was a small brightness is now a flood of orange and red and heat. A wall of flame is spreading around us with the speed of a dam bursting, impossibly fast.

"Come on!" Mari yanks my hand, and we begin to run. The flames lick the trees as we reach them, low branches bursting into a dazzling orange blaze. I steal a glance over my shoulder. Smoke is rising like mist, but I see a white shirt darting after us, not far behind. My lungs tighten as more smoke snakes through my nostrils.

Though we are running as fast as we can, the flames are running faster. They dart from grass to branch to tree like spirits, growing hungrier and opening their flaming mouths wide, as though they will swallow the whole world and everyone in it. The noise is crackling, cracking, the dry wood popping as it blisters and breaks. My chest heaves, stinging from a stitch and the smoke, and Mari is yelling, urging me on.

At last we are ahead of the fire and, coughing, we break through the thin strip of forest. The air is like walking through a waterfall, fresh and bracing. The children are already gathering, and some of them cry out as we emerge. Datu drags us clear, Kidlat trying to help, pulling on my trousers. Sister Teresa pushes her way to the front while Mari retches beside me. Kidlat is running his fingers over my face, frowning, as if checking whether I'm hurt.

"I'm all right, Kidlat," I rasp. "I didn't get burned."

"What's happened? Are you all right?" The nun drops to her knees beside Mari, staring at the blazing trees.

"Mr. . . . Zamora . . . ," gasps Mari.

"He did this?" Sister Teresa spits out the words. "Where is he?"

I look around. He is not here. He has not followed us. Mari and I look at each other, then stare in horror as a burning branch crashes to the ground.

"He was right behind us—" I start.

"He's in the forest?" Sister Teresa leaps to her feet. Ignoring Luko's shout of "No, Sister!" and Mayumi's shriek, she flings her habit across her mouth and plunges into the trees. Luko goes to follow her but another branch crashes to the ground in front of him, and Mayumi shrieks again, pulling him away.

Everything is a confusion of red: faces sweating and glinting, lit by the terrible fire, a heat so strong it feels as though it is singeing my hair. I count slowly to keep from panicking. *One. Two. Three. If she is out by ten, it is fine. Seven. Eight. If she is out by twelve, it is fine. Eleven. Twelve. I meant twenty...*

Although the fire is roaring, it feels very far away, like hearing a storm from the bottom of the sea. The seconds keep passing. *Twenty-one. Twenty-two.* The older boys are hovering at the edge of the forest, trying to see through the fire and billowing black smoke. Finally, after the longest moments, Datu cries out, "They're there!"

A strange shape appears through the smoke.

"Help her!" cries Mayumi.

The shape materializes into Mr. Zamora, leaning heavily on the nun, who has wrapped him in her habit to protect him against the flames. Some of the boys run forward and take Mr. Zamora's limp frame from Sister Teresa, who emerges gasping and spluttering, her eyes rolling, her face streaked with soot. Her wimple is aflame and she claws at it. Luko drags her clear of the smoldering fallen branches.

"Water. Get her water!" Luko shouts, helping her tear off the burning cloth. I force myself upright, head thrumming, and sit watching as Mayumi runs for water.

Under the wimple Sister Teresa's hair is thick and a rich auburn, shining in the firelight, not gray as I'd always supposed. But it is falling out in great clumps, singed in places. Her forehead and neck are blistered and she moans. Her lungs sound

141

as if they are full of fluid, not smoke. Mayumi returns with water, and before long a group of townspeople come running, a water cart following. They must have seen the fire from town. They set up a chain of buckets, doing their best to douse the flames, but none of us is watching the fire. All our attention is focused on Sister Teresa. Luko tries to get her to sit up, but her eyes roll back as she collapses.

"We have to get her to a doctor!" shouts Luko. "I'll take her on Tildie—there's no time to wait for a cart. Someone see to him." He nods at Mr. Zamora, then lifts Sister Teresa.

Kidlat makes his way uncertainly to the collapsed man. Mari has finally stopped coughing, and she also drags herself to Mr. Zamora. I watch Kidlat lower his ear to the man's mouth. Mr. Zamora looks more insect-like than ever, his limbs cricked out.

"Do his lungs sound clear?" asks Mari flatly. Kidlat nods. Mari's mouth sets in a grim line. "Go and get some water, Kidlat. Ami, a rag to clean his face."

Around us it looks like a battlefield, everyone scattered about. The fire has taken what it can from the trees and is dying back slowly. I tear a strip from Mr. Zamora's shirt and wet it in the bucket Kidlat brings, sponging the worst of the soot from the man's face.

Suddenly his eyelids snap back, eyes horribly bloodshot against his ash-gray skin. My face inches from his, he stares so hard at me—no, through me—it is as if his gaze is peeling back my skin. I tense. He smells like sour milk, and soot. His jaw works as he tries to sit up.

"Get away from me, leper."

Mari pushes him back down, hard. His eyes roll and he falls back, panting.

My heart thumps, its pulse heavy in my temple. I drop the shirt and stumble past the water chain toward the orphanage. Luko and Sister Teresa are gone, but more people are arriving from town with more buckets. I hurry inside and collapse on my bed, listening to the shouts and the sloshing of water.

"Ami?" It is as though I have lain here for a thousand years by the time Mari's weight dips the end of the bed. My body feels like it's made of stone, fossilized. I imagine myself sinking down, down, down, through the bed, the floor, into the ground. Mari pulls me up with an enormous tug, and we hold each other in a darkness thick as a cloak after the burning brightness of the fire.

"Do you think Sister Teresa will be all right?" I say finally. Tears are running hotly down my face. Mari pulls back, wiping her cheeks. Her skin shines in the gloom.

"I don't know. She looked bad. Her neck was all burned." She shudders.

"They should lock him up. She might have died. *We* might have—"

"But we didn't," she says fiercely. "And you got your *nanay*'s letter, didn't you?"

I had forgotten, but now I draw it out from my pocket, crumpled but intact. I hesitate. It is not until Mari says, "Ami?" and touches my shoulder that I realize I am holding my breath.

The envelope is thinner than the last one, and when I open it, there is only one sheet of paper. Instantly I know that I was right—there is something wrong. Nanay has written only three lines, and they wave and twist across the paper.

Ami, my child. I have been admitted to the hospital but you must not worry. It is only a complication. I think of you every day. I love you.

Below it are six more lines, but they are not in Nanay's handwriting.

Dearest Ami, your mother's condition is worse than she wishes you to know. I have written to Mr. Zamora requesting special dispensation for you to visit. I am with her as much as possible, and Capuno is there otherwise. We all love you, and hope you can come home soon. Bondoc

"Ami?"

I hear Mari as though through water. I slide off the bed and the ground spins beneath my knees. I have to put my hands

144

down in front of me and hang my head to stop my vision blurring.

"Ami," Mari says again, putting her hand gently on my back and rubbing up and down. I shrug her off and scuttle backward. Her touch is too close to what Nanay used to do when I woke from heaving oceans and night demons, or worlds without her. Worlds without her were the worst.

"Ami, tell me what's wrong." Mari is talking close to my ear, but her words are breaking over me like water. My breath is catching in my throat. I can't get it out and in fast enough. I can't think.

I put a thumb in each ear and spread my fingers hard over my eyes and on my temples. The pressure and quiet focus me. My heart beats a drum in my ears.

For all the excitement of a new place and a new friend, I know at last what some part of me knew all along, even when I sat with Nanay talking about days passing easily, and lines bringing us closer, like steps. I cannot leave her, no matter what the doctors and the notices say. I will not.

When I take my hands away from my face, my heart is beating steadily again, and my head feels clear and certain. The other girls pour into the dormitory, asking us what happened, but Mari is watching me closely. There is something wild in her eyes, setting her irises alight.

Mayumi stands in the doorway, her eyes wide as a startled deer's. "Bed, girls," she says in a cracked voice. "Please, no arguing tonight."

Mari squeezes my hand. "Send me a message." She hurries past the gathering girls and upstairs, head down. As I settle into bed, ignoring the others' whispered questions, the beginnings of a plan begin to itch my palms.

It takes a long time for the dormitory to go silent. The smell of woodsmoke hangs in the air as I wait for the others to sleep. Finally, it is safe to reach for a piece of paper. The string is already waiting outside.

I scribble two sentences.

Mari, I need your help. I have to get back to Culion.

I tie the message onto the string and tug lightly. It begins to rise immediately, but still I will it quicker. Finally the string waves at the window. *How?*

I take a deep breath and write four letters. *Boat.*

The Secret

We are woken by Mayumi, and for a moment I think that she has been left in charge, and that Mr. Zamora has gone. But at ten sharp, he emerges from his hut as normal, as though nothing has happened, despite the courtyard being churned to mud with the water spilled from the buckets. When he speaks, his voice is raspy from the smoke.

"Morning, children," he says, and leers cheerily. "Sister Teresa has been taken to a hospital on the mainland, and Luko is accompanying her. As for the troublemakers who started the fire . . ." He pauses, and fixes his bloodshot eyes on Mari and me. I glare back. "They will be relocated to workhouses as soon as I receive a suitable placement for them from the government." Shock lances through me, and Mari grips my hand.

"He's blaming us for the fire?" she hisses, but I don't care about that. I care about what he said next: a workhouse?

He holds up a piece of paper. "I am sending the request now, and expect to have a reply within a week. They will be relocated separately, of course." He smirks, then places the letter in his breast pocket and starts down the hill.

My hate has crystallized: it sits in my chest, hard and shining. Useful. He thinks he's won, but all he's done is given me strength. A week, and we'll be gone, but together, and not to workhouses. Mari and I head for the cliff.

The forest is reduced to scorched trunks, and we run to avoid the cinders burning our feet.

"I've already thought it all through," she says. "We can salvage some materials from behind the outbuilding—they left plenty of wood and nails—and Luko should have any tools we need. The main problem will be waterproofing, but as long as the boat isn't too badly damaged, I'm sure we can fix it. We'll need oars, of course. How long did you say it took to get here?"

"About two hours."

"Of course it will take longer than that to sail there. Maybe half a day."

"How will we know the wind is right?"

"We keep an eye on Siddy, of course."

"And if the wind isn't in our favor?"

"We row."

"I'm not sure we could row there."

"We can. It'll just take a long time. But if the current helps us—"

I stop in the middle of the path. "You seem to know exactly what to do."

"I've been planning on fixing the boat for a long time. The only thing that stopped me was I had nowhere to go. And no one to go with."

Warmth floods through me. All I can think to say is "Thank you."

She rolls her eyes. "Thank me when we get it floating."

"You don't have to come, you know."

Her face falls. "You want me to go to the workhouse?"

"Of course not."

"Do you not want me to come with you?"

"Of course I do."

"And can you sail? Do knots?"

I shake my head.

"That's settled, then."

Climbing down the narrow path involves a lot of controlled falling on my part. I snatch at tufts of grass and send pebbles scattering. Mari is a lot more graceful than I am, though she uses only one hand. When we reach the spit of sand, she is barely panting. The red-painted boat sits just below the waterline in the shallows, mast arrowing up, tied to a stake by a length of stinking green rope. It looks more like a fishing canoe than a rowing boat, and I know this is a good thing, because they are made to be light and strong, carried to and from the water every day.

"Here it is!" She makes a *Ta-da* movement with her hand. "First job, pull it out."

It is not an easy job. Though the boat looks light, sand has filled the bottom and made it heavy as stone. I see instantly why it has sunk—a long graze near the lip of the hull where it must have scraped a rock.

"We need to tilt it," says Mari. "Tip it over to get the sand out, then we can pull it ashore."

We roll up our trousers and wade in. I take a firm grip on the underside of the boat. It is rough with barnacles and I wince as they scrape my fingers. Mari joins me, hooking her shoulder under the lip of the boat.

"On three. One . . . two . . . three!"

We heave. The boat rocks minutely. Mari counts to three again and again. Each time we strain so hard we sink, sending the sand around our feet swirling. Slowly, achingly, it begins to shift. "Keep going!" cries Mari. I push and push until finally, with a great rush of water, the boat comes unstuck and rolls.

Sand pours out, and Mari sloshes around the other side to steady the boat and make sure it doesn't turn all the way over and smash the mast. The boat begins to lift slightly, with its damaged side up out of the water, and for the first time since reading Nanay's letter, I feel a small seed of hope lodge next to the worry in my stomach.

"Now you go to that side and pull," Mari orders, pointing to the front of the boat. "I'll push."

This part is easier, with the seal of the ocean already broken. We drag it clear of the tidemark and collapse on the sand. The boat sags sideways.

"Now what?" I pant.

"Now we steal."

Mr. Zamora refuses to break his writing routine to keep an eye on us, and so Mayumi is left to control us as best she can. I feel sorry for her, but her soft approach means Mari and I have plenty of time to work on the boat. The other children also make things easier, because without a schedule to occupy them, the boys also ransack the woodpile for material to build tree houses and forts. It is easy enough for Mari and me to take what we need, which is not as much as I'd feared. The hull of our boat is virtually hole-free, and we patch up the crack at the lip as best we can. We steal a rusty bucket from Mayumi's cleaning cupboard for bailing.

Aside from shaking off Kidlat when he tries to follow us, the sail presents the greatest challenge. A single bedsheet lets the wind weave right through, and even with two it barely flutters. I steal three more when it is my turn to do the laundry, and we layer all five, one over the other, and stand with them stretched between us at the cliff edge. The wind shuttles across and catches in the sheet, and Mari is dragged off her feet.

"I think that will work!" She laughs, brushing mud off her knees.

After three days, the boat floats at the end of its green

rope. After five days, we have made three oars out of poles and boards bound together—Mari insisted on a spare.

"What shall we call it?" she asks.

"What do you mean?"

"All boats need names," she says. "It's good luck."

We both go silent, thinking. Finally Mari snaps her fingers. "I've got it. *Lihim.*"

"Secret?"

"Our secret." She smiles.

On the sixth day Mr. Zamora returns from town with a letter. He brandishes it at Mari and me at dinner. "You may want to take today to say your goodbyes. I've had letters from two workhouses keen for children—good for sliding into spaces between machinery." His face seems more skull than skin as he walks away to his hut, whistling.

"Why are you smiling?" says Tekla to Mari, her voice harsh. "Those places are horrible. You could lose a hand—oh, wait."

Some of the other girls giggle but Mari looks right at Tekla. "You should be kinder. Your face will be as vile as his soon enough." She leans her head into mine. "First light, yes?"

I nod, looking around the fire. No one seems much upset by our leaving. Only Kidlat is watching me, though even he has pulled away the past few days. I suppose if you push someone away enough, they will stop trying. The small pang in my chest is swallowed by determination. We are going to get back to Nanay: we will.

I barely sleep, and as soon as light gleams from the courtyard through the shutters, I hear the creak of a floorboard above my head. I creep past the sleeping girls to where Mari is waiting with a pillowcase in the courtyard, her face alight with excitement. She points at Siddy. Siddy, in turn, is pointing toward the front of the orphanage.

Without a word to each other, we snatch as much fruit as we can from Luko's stores by the fire pit, and take off at a run. The forest is blackened and quiet, the ground ashes, the smell of woodsmoke still hanging in the early-morning air.

I hesitate at the top of the cliff, my heart pounding. The shadow of Culion Island is pinkening in the sunrise. It seems an impossible distance, and I am afraid of what we will find there. But then Mari takes my hand and squeezes it.

"Come on."

We plunge down the path and I land in a bundle by Mari's feet.

"We did it!" I cry, but Mari is not looking at me. Her eyes are wide, staring up the slope behind us. I turn. This is one thing we haven't planned for.

There, making his unsteady way down the twilight cliff, is Kidlat.

The Crossing

Stop!" I shout, but he is already halfway, reaching the dangerous scree toward the base of the cliff. Mari shoves her pillowcase at me and clambers up to meet him. I expect her to turn him around but she helps him navigate down.

"What're you doing?"

"We don't have time to take him back," says Mari, regaining her breath. "And we can't leave him here. He'll have to come."

I stare down at the silent child.

"It's all right," I say softly. It looks like he is biting down on his thumb rather than sucking it. I reach out a hand and lay it lightly on the crook of his small arm.

Kidlat's eyes flick rapidly from Mari to me, his breathing fast. I move closer and lay my other hand on his back, rubbing gently. Mari sits down too, and slowly, slowly, Kidlat's breaths calm. He allows me to guide his hand out of his mouth and I see the tooth marks around the base of his thumb. His eyes fix on mine, and I know Mari is right. We have to go before anyone notices we're missing, and it would be nearly impossible for him to climb back up on his own.

"Listen, Kidlat. We're going on a trip. You're going to have to do exactly as we say, all right?"

He nods.

"At least he's only small," says Mari.

I bite back any meanness, though I am angry that he's followed us. I want to get to Nanay as quickly as possible.

Kidlat sits on the beach as we ready *Lihim*, tying on the bedsheet sail and guiding the oars into their grooves. Mari helps Kidlat aboard and takes an oar in her good hand.

"Ready?" I say.

She nods, her pale skin flushed. I push us out into deeper water. When I am up to my chest, I kick my legs hard and haul myself over the side of the boat. It rocks precariously, and some water seeps in through the patched crack below the lip, but soon it rights itself.

"We need to get clear of the cliffs," says Mari, nodding at the empty sail. "They're stopping the wind. We'll have to row."

Mari holds out her right wrist and I bind it to the oar so she can use both arms. I sit next to her and take up the other oar.

"Kidlat, you can be in charge of the pail. If any water comes over the side—"

"Or *through* the side, or the bottom—"

"*Thank you,* Mari," I snap before turning back to the silent boy. "Scoop it out, all right?"

He takes up the rusty bucket and begins to fill and tip. Mari and I start to row. It is hard from the first moment, and as the moments add up, I pray silently that the wind is still blowing to Culion when we clear the bay. Mari grunts with the effort, the string cutting white into her arm. After a few long minutes, the mast creaks. We turn and see the sail billow. I hold my breath, and the wind seems to too. Then the sail fills. The boat begins to move.

Mari lifts her oar clear of the water and unties the string. She throws down the wood and jumps to her feet.

"We did it. We're going! We're really going! Come on, *Lihim!*"

The boat rocks again and she stumbles to her knees, laughing. Kidlat is smiling widely, waving his little arms in the air. We edge out into the open ocean.

The sea is not calm like it was the day of our first crossing. Or perhaps it is because we are in a boat that is so much smaller that the waves feel bigger. After only a few minutes, Kidlat goes pale and uses the bucket to be sick into. Mari rinses it out and takes over bailing out the water seeping in through holes that are only noticeable because of the bubbles springing from them. But it is not an impossible amount of water, and I know from our journey to the orphanage that it is not an impossible distance, either. Mari seems in a good mood, and I suppose that sailing a boat is making her think of her father.

I crawl to the front of the boat, ducking under the sail so I can watch the boat cut the water. I think of the people who owned it, who hauled nets full of fish aboard and painted it red and finally left it tied in a shallow cove. Where have they gone? Perhaps they hoped someone would find and fix it someday. Perhaps Mari and I were always meant to find it.

But that would mean I was always meant to come to the orphanage, which in turn would mean Nanay was always meant to be sick, and I don't like to think that. That's the problem with believing there's a reason for everything—you have to take the good with the bad. Nanay taught me the word for it: *tadhana,* the invisible force that makes things happen outside our control. Like earthquakes or shipwrecks. Or falling in love.

Mari comes to join me in the bow of the boat. She holds out one of the oranges she stole from Luko. "Breakfast time."

I peel it and we share the segments, spitting the pips over the waves. The wind carries them farther than we could throw, and I think of that same wind blowing ahead, all the way home.

"Is Kidlat all right?"

Mari shrugs. "I think so. He's sleeping."

"What're we going to do when we get to Culion? Hand him over or ..."

"We'll have to bring him with us," says Mari. "There's no way to make sure he's safe without handing ourselves over too. They'll put us on the first boat back."

"How can we be sure we're going the right way?"

"Siddy said."

"But the wind changes, doesn't it? So what if he's not saying this way anymore? What if we go off course, or hit another island, or—"

Mari holds her hand up to my mouth. "Ami, trust me."

Trusting her has nothing to do with the wind or the sea, but her light, clear eyes fix on me and I feel a bit calmer. I lean to peer around the sail. The wind hits me full in the face, making tears start in my eyes.

Kidlat is curled up with his thumb in his mouth. Behind him, our cliff is already a smudge, a raised line as high as my finger. On the other horizon there are only waves, small hills rolling on and on. The sea is not light blue anymore—up close it is a night sky, opaquely navy. I think of all the things beneath us, the fish and the coral and the sharks. *Trust me.* The mast groans and rasps as the wind cracks in our sail.

Mari is sitting sideways with her knees drawn up to her chest so she fits in the narrow hull. I slide down beside her.

"You're still worrying," she says. "Your face is all scrunchy."

"How are you *not* worried?"

"It's an adventure. It's exciting." Her eyes shine. "I've never had one before."

"But what if the monsoon comes early? What if the clouds roll over and—"

"And what if the sea opens up and swallows us! What if a

huge ship comes through and snaps our boat in half! What if we fall overboard and forget how to swim!"

"Exactly. I suppose we could pray?"

Mari wrinkles her nose. "You don't believe in all that, do you?"

"All what?"

"Praying. God." She says it like Nanay does.

"I don't know."

She shakes her head, exasperated. "Ami, if you always worried about the worst that could happen, you'd never *do* anything. We'd still be in that orphanage, or on a ship to somewhere else, probably not the same place as each other. But we're here, going to see your *nanay*. We're *doing* it. We've gone. So stop worrying. It's too late. And if any of those things do happen, we'll deal with them, all right?"

"All right."

"Tell me about her." Mari's voice is level again. "About your *nanay*."

I have spent weeks not doing this. Not allowing my mind to fully turn to her. But now I reach for everything I know and let it fall out, all jumbled up and in the wrong order. I tell her about the butterfly house, about star catching and our stories. I tell her about Nanay facing down Mr. Zamora without her scarf, and Mari lets out a low whistle.

"She sounds brilliant. She sounds brave."

"She's not brave exactly," I say. "It's more that she doesn't care what other people think. She didn't care if Mr. Zamora thought she was strange-looking."

"That's brave, though," says Mari. Her voice is soft. "If my parents had stopped worrying about what other people thought, I'd still be with them."

"What do you mean?"

"I mean your *nanay* is brave," Mari says, brushing off my question like she has every other question. "Tell me one of her stories."

But my eyes have fixed on something past Mari's head. The small hills of the waves beyond waves are growing higher. Growing higher, and not shrinking.

"Look!"

And Mari turns her light eyes toward the hills of Culion.

We wake Kidlat and share another orange. The sun is at its highest point, and I cannot believe that it has taken only half a day to sight home. We play at guessing how many hours it will take to reach the shore, Kidlat holding up pudgy fingers, changing his mind every minute.

Mari and I are laughing so hard at him holding up one finger that it takes a moment to realize he is pointing. Too late, I see the jag of coral, mouthing up like a fang as the waves fall away. Mari scrambles for an oar and manages to jab us away, but the sail is carrying us fast toward another. I look down and see that the water is aglow with coral, red and pink, and the water foaming white over it. The reef.

"Help me!" Kidlat hurries to help Mari steady her oar. I grab the other and join them in heaving us away from the shallows, but the wind is straining to pull us back.

"The sail!" Mari shouts. "We have to take it down."

My fingers scrabble at the knots binding the sheets to the mast. The boat jolts and I drop to my knees, feeling rather than hearing the scrape of the underside against coral. Mari's right hand is making it hard for her to grip the oar, and though Kidlat's little arms shake with effort, they aren't able to push us away. The blade of the oar catches and Mari makes a grab for it, almost falling overboard. The oar falls away and I snatch it back up, knuckles grazing on a vicious orange frill. The blade is snapped and I stab at the sail, tearing through sheet after sheet until finally the wind gushes through and we slow, rocking but no longer scraping.

Mari is cradling her right wrist and I can see that the skin is pink and sore-looking. Kidlat is on his knees, panting, and I feel a sudden rush of heat. My heart punches at my chest as I throw down the broken oar. Kidlat flinches into Mari.

"Ami, what—" Mari starts.

"You . . . you broke the oar."

"I couldn't get it free in time. We have a spare."

"You broke the oar and now we have no sail!" My shout shocks me as much as her. I cannot remember the last time

161

my voice scraped my throat like this, the last time my hands balled into fists. The last time I wanted to hurt someone. "You stupid, stupid—" I round on Kidlat. "And you! Couldn't you have just shouted? Couldn't you have warned us? You're not a baby anymore, use your stupid mouth!"

"Ami!" Mari stands, moving Kidlat behind her. "Stop it!"

"You said to trust you, and look. Look! We're never going to get there—"

"It wasn't anyone's fault—"

"You're useless, both of you. Useless. Look at you—"

Mari shoves me, hard. I fall backward, hitting my grazed hand. The sharp shock of the pain brings all the heat rushing to it, flushing out the anger and making it shrink into shame.

"Mari, I—"

"*Never* talk to me like that again." Mari brings her face down level with mine. There are hot patches of red on her pale cheeks, and the high midday sun glares through her hair, turning it into a halo. She looks like a terrible angel. *"Never."*

"I'm sorry." Tears scald my cheeks. "I don't know why . . ."

Mari pulls me toward her and for a moment I think she is going to hit me, but instead she hugs me, harder than she shoved me. After a few moments Kidlat shuffles over and the three of us sit in a tight huddle until I feel water begin to seep up my legs.

"We'd better bail," says Mari, and reaches for the bucket. Kidlat holds out his hands for it but Mari shakes her head. "I think Ami should do it, to say sorry."

Mari and Kidlat take down the remnants of the sail and rip through my gashes so the sheets are in half. They set to re-tying the layers together while I scoop out the calf-high water. I am glad of the task. The words I said seem to have left grazes on my tongue. It feels swollen and poisonous, and my stomach churns with points of cooling anger, like shards of glass. I spoke like Mr. Zamora would, or how San did that first day. I bail faster, so my arms ache and my head spins. I will never speak like that again.

We row over the rest of the reef, with Kidlat in front pointing out the safest path. The coral has punctured some holes in the bottom of the boat but we escaped the worst of it. My words have done the most damage. Though Mari is trying not to seem angry with me, I can feel a cool distance stretch between us as we navigate into open water again.

When we are clear, I help Kidlat tie the smaller sail to the mast and it billows feebly. We begin to move again, far slower than before, but Culion's toothlike hills are closer than ever. Coron is out of sight beyond the horizon behind us. I take up the oars and help the sail guide us shoreward.

"You don't have to do that, Ami," says Mari. "You should rest."

But I do have to do it. I'm not done saying sorry yet.

The Forest

*S*omehow, it is always dusk when you approach.

That's what Nanay always told me, and now twilight is falling when I see the lights, strung out against the forest like rosary beads. Like a necklace. The *Sano* port, glinting ahead and to the right. My arms shake but my head fills with a strange lightness.

I have had to row since the hills started to tower and shrink the wind until the sail emptied entirely. Mari and Kidlat are curled up asleep and I am glad Mari's eyes are closed so I cannot see the hurt in them anymore. There is a boat hunched in the harbor but there doesn't appear to be anyone around.

The tide seems to be carrying us in, and I guide the boat as best I can toward a small cove to the left of the harbor. The necklace winks out of sight as the scraping of rocks jerks Mari and Kidlat awake. Mari looks around. Beyond the rocky beach, the forest sways darkly.

"Ami, you did it." Mari looks at me and smiles. The knot in my chest unravels.

We take up our pillowcases and splosh into the shallows. It is not quite so shallow for Kidlat and he clings to Mari's legs until we reach the beach. The solid ground feels tricksy under my feet, untethered as though it were the ocean. We sit a moment to steady ourselves. My mouth is dry and the orange segment Mari offers sings over my tongue. I watch the narrow shape of our boat bobbing against the rocks. The tide will take it out, unless it sinks without anyone to bail. Perhaps someone else will find it and fix it all over again.

"Goodbye, *Lihim*," I murmur.

"We'd better go," says Mari.

Walking in the dark should feel like an adventure, but all I can think about is how big the forest is and how small we are in it. The rains will be here soon, the clouds thickening and spilling, washing the air clean. For now, the night sky feels heavy above us, our breath thick.

We cross the road that brought Kidlat and me to the harbor and keep to the shadows so we can go uphill if we hear anyone coming. It should be easy enough to follow the road from a safe distance. The road that goes all the way to Culion Town. The forested hills loom above us, muffled and watchful. The ground is firm and branch-covered, and it would be impossible to see a snake in the shadows. Rosita used to say to let matters be and the things that matter will take care of themselves. It seems a silly thing to think and I'm not sure I believe her, but it is rude to think ill of the dead, so I decide to stop worrying about what is snake and what is shadow.

Mari and I are silent until we reach the river. Kidlat is too, but he is always silent. I remember the river crossing the path close to the end of our cart ride, and feel a fluttering in my stomach. We are moving so much more slowly than I'd imagined. A day instead of a couple of hours for the crossing, and how many more hours to reach here? The trees are set back, so the moon beams down strong and silver. I untie the basin from my back and use it to collect water so we can drink. The taste of garlic and shrimp has still not entirely faded. The forest is motionless around us, but not quiet. We can hear frogs, the faint bubble of fish in the water, insects clicking at each other.

"We should have brought a net," I say. "Or some lines."

"I have something better. My party trick. I'll show you I'm not useless." Mari holds up her limp hand and wiggles her eyebrows so I can tell she's teasing, but it still sends shame lancing through me. "Grab that." She points to a flat stone nearby. "Hold it up. And be ready."

I don't ask what for. She lies on her belly by the low bank, and lets her hand dangle in the current. Kidlat leans in to watch too. For a long while nothing happens, but I don't interrupt. Her gaze has a beamlike focus. Then something glints by her fingers. It starts to nibble at the skin. I suck in my breath, but Mari doesn't flinch.

More tiny fish gather, but it is only when a larger silver-green tilapia begins to pick them off that Mari brings her other hand down fast, scooping under the fish and flipping it out of the water, onto the bank. The fish lands two yards away from me, flapping and gasping.

"Get it, Ami!"

I mean to, but I've never killed something like this. I've only ever collected meat already parceled in brown paper from Rosita's, or dropped crabs into oil and not had to watch.

"Ami!"

The fish is flopping its way closer to the water, its panic taking it up in great arcs around my ankles. Mari stands up and grabs the stone from me. I hold on to it a little longer than I should, hoping that the fish will make it back to the water.

The stone falls and Mari rolls her eyes at me as she kicks it away from the fish. "We almost lost it."

The underside of the stone has a dark smear and I don't want to look at the fish, but can see it at the corner of my vision, twitching limply in Mari's hand. She has picked it up by the tail and hits it against the stone and the twitching stops. I feel as if I'm about to cry. Kidlat is already sniffling.

"Did you have to do that?" I say, and my voice is angrier than I want it to be.

"What?"

"Hit it again!"

Mari hooks her finger under the gill and tilts her head at me like a quizzical bird. "It was dying. It was in pain. I meant to kill it with the stone, first time. It's kinder that way."

I sniff. Something is dripping from the fish, making a dull splatting noise on the stone.

Mari holds it out to me apologetically. "I can't prepare this on my own, Ami. Can you help me?"

Her face is so worried and so kind that I feel embarrassed. I nod firmly. "Yes, of course. I'm sorry, I don't know—"

"No, I'm sorry. I thought you'd have seen that before. It's—it's just food, Ami. It's because we need food."

"I know that," I say, flushing.

"There's going to be more blood when we gut it."

"It's not the blood," I say. And it's not. It's the death.

She smiles hesitantly, then kneels and begins to rinse the fish in the quick-moving water. When she holds it out to me, it looks as clean as when it came out of the river alive. It looks like the fish Nanay used to buy from Bondoc, that I helped her prepare a hundred times before. My throat feels a little less dry. I wash the dark stain off the stone and take the cold, firm body in both hands. I place it on the flat surface while Kidlat and Mari sift through the stones at the bank, searching for one that has not been smoothed by the water.

Kidlat hands me a sharp oblong stone, and holding the fish steady by its tail, I run the edge up its side. The scales come off like tiny mirrors, speckling the rock and making my fingers glint. I slice the fins off and lay them to one side. Then, hooking my finger through a gill, I split the belly, running the flint down so it opens and I can scoop out the insides. Mari looks away at this bit, and I'm surprised, seeing as she was so brisk with the stone.

The flint isn't sharp enough to fillet the tilapia neatly, so once I've rinsed the fleshy inside, we take turns stripping the meat from the bones with our fingers. It's fresh enough to be eaten raw, though it doesn't taste very good. I try not to let my mind wander to the meal on the beach with Nanay, or even Luko's boiling pot and rice.

As I swallow my last mouthful, Mari nudges me. Kidlat is curled up on the ground, fast asleep.

"We should wake him," I say.

"Couldn't we let him sleep a moment? I'm too tired to carry him."

I look down at the tiny frame and sigh. Every moment we waste sleeping is another moment before we get to Nanay. But I can't bear to wake Kidlat. I look along the river to where it disappears back into the thicket, and wonder if I should suggest I go on alone. But the darkness is suddenly terrifying.

"A couple of hours won't hurt," I say, and suddenly my legs begin to ache as if they have only just realized how much walking they have done. Mari nods and curls up too, her back against Kidlat's. I lie down on his other side, facing the river. The water whispers over the rocks; the insects click.

The Horses

Mari is standing before me, but something is wrong. Her hair is shining too brightly, her eyes are too large.

Mari, I say, but my voice comes out in bubbles through the air. She holds out her arms to me.

Ami, can you help me?

Two limp fish are growing from her wrists, their eyes flat and dead in the moonlight. I back away as she advances. Suddenly she fades and Nanay is there, waist-high in fast-flowing water. Her mouth opens and closes out of time with her words.

Ami, can you help me?

I can't get to her in time. The river is rising, and as I reach out, all I scoop up is water, and I'm calling her ...

Ami, can you hear me?

Mari's voice is back, and Nanay is fading into a slow light.

"Ami, can you hear me?"

I am beginning to feel my body again, drawing itself up around me as if through mud. Nanay is gone.

"Ami, wake up!"

I open my eyes and Mari is there, really there, in a colorless, uncertain morning light, nudging me. My hand is trailing in the river, numb with cold. I pull it out and sit up, shaking my head to rid it of the images.

"You were having a bad dream," she says. Kidlat is clinging to her tunic, his eyes frightened.

"It's all right. I was asleep," I say, more to myself than to him. "It was just a dream."

But it felt true, in the way that horrible dreams do, though I can see for myself that Nanay is not there and Mari has one hand that looks like mine, and another that is nothing like a fish.

"We should go," she says, holding out a piece of jackfruit. The sweetness hits my nostrils and turns my stomach but my mouth is horribly dry. I take it and eat as Mari pockets the fish-gutting flint and brings me the basin to retie on my back. As I do so, the vision of Nanay waist-deep in water rises and sticks to my skin, and it must show in my face because Mari pulls Kidlat along in my wake without another word.

The heat is increasing every minute, the air full of that thickness that means the rains are another day closer. The sky is a smooth gray through the trees above us, the sun's light flattened across the tops of the clouds that formed in the night. I focus on the river, the way it is flowing from Culion Town, and how every step upriver is a step closer to Nanay. I try very hard not to think of her in pain, in the hospital, surrounded by strangers from the Places Outside.

"Ami, can we slow down a bit?"

I turn around and see Mari and Kidlat far behind. I thought I had only walked a short way, but I can no longer see the clearing where we slept, only more and more branches and trunks and beams of sunlight pushing down like fingers through the shade. I stop and take a few deep gulps of air as they catch up.

My body feels tight, and my hands are shaking. I bunch them into fists so Mari won't see, but of course she notices. I liked her watchfulness when I met her, but right now it feels like nosiness. Kidlat seems to have decided she is his new favorite, and something approaching anger wells inside me. When we arrived on Coron, it was my hand he reached for. Now Mari is shielding him slightly, as if I'm a snake. She barely knows him. And why did he follow us in the first place? We could be moving far faster without him.

I bite my teeth together hard to stop any of the thoughts coming out, but Mari is looking at me with her light eyes as though she can see inside my head. I turn away without a word and carry on along the river, shortening my stride and feeling angrier with every step. I wish I were alone, I wish I could run ahead without having to worry about a five-year-old keeping up ...

Stop, I tell myself firmly. It's not their fault. No one's to blame except Mr. Zamora, who took me away, and the government that sent him, and, more than either of those, it's what is in my *nanay*'s blood, in her skin, taking her piece by piece.

I slow my pace a little more and fall into step beside Mari. Kidlat is holding her hand on the other side but she links her arm through mine and squeezes.

"It's going to be all right, Ami," she says fiercely. "We're going to make good time. We're not going to be caught. We're going to make it back."

She stops there, because she cannot promise how Nanay will be when we arrive. I return the squeeze with the crook of my elbow.

We only stop when Kidlat's stomach starts to growl loudly enough we can hear it over the river and our footsteps. Mari finds some more jackfruit and we eat one each, the juice dripping down our chins. The flies begin hovering about our faces, so we wash them in the river. The water is cool and clean and I think briefly how it is a shame I am only just learning about these forests now, when all I want is to be out of them, back at home.

Kidlat has still not said a word but he seems calmer. He seems to know that it is important we keep going as he matches our pace. But as the hours pass and the sun reaches the top of the sky, he slows down, and by midafternoon we are taking one step to every three of his. His bottom lip begins to tremble and we stop.

"I could carry him?" says Mari, looking at my anxious face, but I shake my head. The need to get back to Nanay is mine, and it is my fault we are going so fast. I untie the basin from my back and retie it around Mari, then crouch down for Kidlat to climb onto my back. He wraps his arms around my shoulders as Mari begins to sing in a soft, clear voice, a song I've never heard before. The tune is gentle but with an undercurrent of sadness, and I don't understand the words.

"What language is that?"

"Spanish. My parents used to sing it to me." She smiles sadly. "That's one of the reasons I think they loved me. You don't sing to someone you don't love, do you?"

I shake my head. "And they taught you fishing and boats. I'm sure your parents loved you. I'm sure they only gave you away because they had no choice." Like Nanay had to let me go.

"I hope so." Mari looks away.

"And it's a lovely song they left you. What does it mean?"

She smiles at me. "If you don't know what it means, how do you know it's lovely? I could be singing 'I hate you and you smell' for all you know."

"Is that what it means?"

She laughs and shakes her head, then sings it again, in Tagalog this time.

Find me a boat and we'll float to the sea,
Come, little one, come, there is so much to be.
The world is so big and there's so much to see,
Come, little one, come and go floating with me.

I join in after the second time and we walk to the rhythm, Kidlat humming tunelessly near my ear. We sing it faster and faster, our pace increasing until we are nearly running and I have to stop and put Kidlat down because I'm laughing so hard I can't breathe.

Then Mari is pressing her hand against my mouth. I choke on a breath and start to cough but she pushes her wrist over her hand and shushes me urgently. I swallow down the cough and listen.

Horses. There are horses nearby, and men talking. I can hear the low burr of their voices, and hooves scuffing the path. We flatten ourselves to the ground, trying not to rustle too much, as three sets of hooves appear through the trunks to our left. I don't know how we have curved so close to the path without noticing. They are far enough away to stop me panicking, but still my heart thumps wildly, as if it is trying to burrow into the ground.

"We would've seen them by now, surely?" says a man's voice I recognize. My skin tingles. Bondoc. "We should turn back, Mr. Zamora."

Kidlat lets out a tiny gasp and I pull him closer, too scared to try to catch sight of Bondoc.

"Maybe we should," says another familiar voice. Dr. Tomas sounds tired. "We've found no trace."

"They are here somewhere!" Mr. Zamora's voice is furious. "I saw them sailing out—"

"How could children sail all that way?" snaps Bondoc impatiently. "If this is a cover-up for something you've done—"

"I've done nothing. You think I'd return to this disgusting island if I knew where—"

There is a scuffling noise.

"Let go!" says Mr. Zamora.

"Bondoc—" Dr. Tomas warns. There is a silence.

"What am I meant to tell Tala?" says Bondoc finally, his voice breaking.

Mari grips my hand tightly. *Tell.* He said "tell." That means she's still alive. A huge lump rises in my throat. I want to laugh and cry all at once.

"That leper woman?" Mr. Zamora's voice is taunting, and I hear another scuffle.

"Bondoc, no!" says Dr. Tomas. "Mr. Zamora, please refrain from saying such th—"

"We're wasting time," says Bondoc. "He must be lying."

"I am not. We should press on."

I press my cheek to the ground so I can see up to their waists. Bondoc's fists are clenching and unclenching. Dr. Tomas is standing between him and Mr. Zamora's thin legs.

Bondoc grunts. "Fine. Let me get some water first."

Beside me I feel Mari slither backward, and Kidlat turns

176

and crawls quickly away. I am slower, still dazed by their mention of Nanay.

"Ami!" hisses Mari, tugging my foot. I come to my senses and move to join them behind the trees but it is too late.

Bondoc's mouth falls open. Then he presses his lips tight and I see tears start in his eyes.

"Hurry up, Bondoc!"

We both jump, and he shouts, "Coming," his voice cracking slightly.

He crouches down and splashes the water so it sounds like drinking as he murmurs, "Ami, thank goodness. Are you well?"

I nod.

"Are the other two with you?"

Another nod.

"You beautiful, brilliant girl." He is shaking. He reaches out across the water and we brush fingertips. "Did you hear? I'm with that awful man. I can't say I've seen you. You're all safe?"

Two more nods, my eyes wide.

"Stay that way. I'll tell her you're coming. You're not far now." He splashes his face to hide his tears, then takes an unfeigned gulp of water from his cupped hand. Then, with a deep breath, he straightens and walks stiffly back in the direction of the others. I blink stupidly after him. Just before he reaches the path, he takes two steps back. His hand comes up in a fast arc, and throws something.

A book of matches from the tavern lands by my feet. By the time I've picked it up, he is swinging himself into his saddle. I see feet kick the horses into action and they ride back the way they came. Mari runs to me from the shelter of the trees.

"Ami!" Her voice sounds feverish. "What happened? What did he say?"

I hold up the book of matches dumbly and she stares. Kidlat comes and kneels beside us, thumb back in his mouth. I clear my throat and answer Mari's questions.

She blows out her cheeks. "You have the luck of the devil, Ami."

I grin, the shock fading, leaving a manic giddiness bubbling in my stomach. "I thought you didn't believe in the devil."

She grins too. "I don't believe in things I can't see, Ami. And I met Mr. Zamora same as you."

I snort and pull her to her feet. I go to lift Kidlat but he shakes his head and begins walking. Mari raises her eyebrows and links her arm through mine. "After you, sir." She makes a low bow, dragging me into it with her. The boy giggles.

Something has lifted from my shoulders. Seeing Bondoc, his gift of matches and his whispered *not far now* are like points of heat on my skin, driving my steps, giving me hope. We don't talk about Nanay or Mari's parents or anything sad. Kidlat and Mari seem to be in a better mood too, so much so that when the moon comes up, Mari suggests we walk through the night.

I want to, but I can tell Kidlat is exhausted, and I don't think I can manage to carry him after so much walking. We stop and set Kidlat to collecting some wood for the fire while Mari and I catch and gut another fish. I manage to drop the stone myself this time, though I have to close my eyes.

I light the small stack of twigs with one of Bondoc's matches. Kidlat wants to try lighting a match, so I let him have two, both of which snap and fall either into the fire or into the river. We watch the flames grow and then shrink to a reddish, glowing heat. We pick absentmindedly at the fish, so by the time the fire is hot enough to cook it, we've eaten it raw. Kidlat is half asleep, so I shift him away from the flames, and Mari rinses the basin in the river.

There's a faint buzzing nearby, and the fire's glow picks out a pale cone hanging in a tree across the river. I swallow hard. Wasps have always scared me, ever since Nanay smoked a nest out from our wall when I was little. It was behind my bed, and at night I could hear them buzzing. I thought I was imagining things until Nanay was stung slapping the broom against the wall outside. They all rose up in a tide and she was lucky to be stung only twice, once on her wrist and again on her neck. She pumped the wall full of smoke and then there were hundreds of dead bodies behind my bed. Rotted to dust now, probably, and all the tunnels empty.

"You all right, Ami?" asks Mari, and I realize I was far away.

"Sort of," I say after a moment's silence.

"Good enough," she says, and curls up next to Kidlat. I lie down on the other side of him and she reaches over the sleeping boy to squeeze my hand. I squeeze hers back and she lets it rest in mine for a long moment before turning over and whispering, "Good night."

I think of *Lihim,* abandoned on the beach, the tide taking our secret and burying it in the sand. Sleep comes choppy as waves.

The Orchard

The air is so hot I am already sweating when my body wakes me up. It feels as though I'm breathing through steam. The sky is that same flat gray as yesterday, and there is no sign of the sun just yet.

The rains are coming very soon. I hope we get to Culion Town before they arrive, but you can never tell. Sometimes they come on blue days, the cloud sweeping over like a tide and opening in a great rush of water that soaks the ground so fast our houses flood before we can build dams, or lay down sand or rushes. Other times they fill the sky so thick and heavy with clouds you think it will fall like a blanket, but instead the rain comes a little at a time, as though it might change its mind at any moment and be sucked back into the sky.

There is no jackfruit for breakfast, so Mari hands out the last of Luko's oranges.

"I never want to eat another orange again," I say, pocketing mine. Mari grins and chomps hers. Her obsession with oranges is a little worrying.

She makes a half-hearted attempt at luring another fish but they are all full from a night of feeding and wary in the morning light. We fill our bellies with water and begin walking. The trees are closing in closer to the bank, so we weave between them, Kidlat trying to skip and giggling when he stumbles. It is good to see him unafraid.

My stomach begins cramping after a couple of hours, and after another hour Kidlat tugs on Mari's hand, gesturing for food. Though we scan the trees for fruit and the ground for roots, all I can see is a thicket of thorny acacias that catch at our tunics and arms. We don't break any branches, though, because *diwata* live in acacias. They are the trees' guardian spirits, who do harm to those who harm their home. When Nanay told me about them, I imagined beautiful women a foot high, draped over branches in orange silk. Now, seeing how sharp the thorns are, all I can think is that the gods must have very thick skin.

A strange smell fills the air as we walk: sweet, cloying and slightly rotten. If I breathe it in too deeply, my head spins and my teeth ache. It is not entirely unpleasant but Mari covers her nose with her tunic. Around a long bend of the river we see something that makes both Mari and me pull up short. Kidlat, walking slightly behind by now, steps on the back of my foot but I barely notice.

Before us is a sudden clearing, the ground covered by a thick, beautiful carpet of green and black and gold. It spreads on either side of the river, which is narrower now and flowing faster, so we must be nearing its source. The threads catch the light and glisten in the high sun. The smell is stronger than ever and I feel my head spinning, my body slow, a bit like how Bondoc described being drunk. Mari swings out an arm before I can step forward.

"What are you doing?" she hisses through her tunic.

I look down at the carpet, except it isn't a carpet anymore. I stumble backward, gasping. Kidlat tries to move out of the way but I trip over him and we collapse in a heap.

A tide of flies and wasps rises from the ground before us, no longer glimmering threads of black and gold, but blur-winged, bulbous-eyed and buzzing. The orange and green colors of the carpet are many fallen mangoes in various states of decay, the smell pungent and sickening. The insects flick across the clearing, disturbed by our presence, before settling again, like a net thrown over the rotting fruit. I see the scuttle of rats. The heat and smell are making me nauseous.

Mari laughs at my stricken face. "What's wrong with you?"

I feel my face prickle with embarrassment. I don't want to tell her what I thought it was. I shrug, and laugh hollowly. Kidlat has wriggled out from under me.

"Yuck."

We both jump and look at him.

"What did you say, Kidlat?" I ask tentatively.

"Yuck. Flies, yuck."

They are the first words he's said in front of us, and Mari snorts with laughter. "Well said, Kidlat!"

"So you can speak!" I exclaim, but Kidlat only shrugs an *of course*. I shake my head wonderingly.

"An excellent choice of first word." Mari grins and points to the edge of the clearing. "We'll need to walk around. You may enjoy the feeling of rotten fruit and flies underfoot, but I don't." She tosses this over her shoulder at me, already striding away.

I take Kidlat's hand and we follow her.

"This must be the mango grove we passed on the way here," I say to him, the idea just occurring to me. This is near where Mr. Zamora dropped the butterflies, and where Datu picked the rotten fruit. I wonder what the children back at the orphanage think of our running away. If they think of us at all. "We're nearly home."

"Home," Kidlat says seriously. "Your *nanay*."

"Yes." My face stretches in such a big smile I feel it might crack. His voice is clear and sweet. I feel a rush of warmth as he looks up at me, smiling so wide his whole face stretches too. Only Nanay has ever made me feel like this before: like a person could be home and safety and everything that mattered. A universe, just like Nanay said Ama was to her.

"And my *nanay*?"

"Yes."

"Ami! Kidlat!" Mari's voice is joyful. "Look!"

She is out of sight. We fight through a thick tangle of acacias, planted—I realize now—to protect the fruit from thieves and trespassers like us. We reach her.

"Look!" she says again, and Kidlat runs forward into the lines of trees ahead of us, laughing happily. The clearing was only the start of the fruit farm. This grove is full of *pitaya*, dragon fruit, with their bright pink-and-green frills only just ripening beneath the canopies of spiny green. Kidlat slices one open across the sharp leaves and runs back to us.

"Hands," he says. We dutifully hold out our palms. He rips the dragon fruit apart and turns the skin inside out so that the fruit drops out, the flesh white and seeded. "Eat."

"Thank you, sir," says Mari, slipping into another low bow. He laughs and goes to fetch more. The fruit is lightly scented, a welcome change from the rotting mangoes, and tastes sweet and clean. After three more my hunger begins to fade, falling to a low ache in the pit of my stomach.

"What a place," says Mari, lying back and stretching like a cat wanting its belly stroked.

"We're so close, Mari," I say, too excited to lie down. "This grove, we passed it on the way. A few miles, I reckon. Maybe three—"

"Must've been abandoned awhile, judging by those mangoes."

"Mmm. Did you hear me?"

"It's a shame, all this waste. And it's so beautiful." She sits up suddenly. "Ami," she says in a low voice, her irises golden, her gaze fixed on me. "Can I ask you something?"

"What?"

Her face is smiling but there is something uncertain in her expression, as if she is nervous or unsure. But of course Mari is never nervous, and definitely never unsure.

"After we get back to Culion Town, and after whatever comes next, can we go back to the forest? Not this forest, necessarily," she adds, waving around her. "But somewhere with trees and flowers and fruit and a river?"

"Why?"

She frowns. "Because it's beautiful. And I like being here—if it weren't for why we're here in the first place."

The thought drops a stone into my chest, because "after" somehow seems sad, or scary. *After whatever comes next.* I don't like most of the options for what is coming next. Mari lies back down.

"Forget it," she says sharply, as though we'd argued. I've opened my mouth without knowing what I'm about to say when we hear Kidlat screech. Mari reacts quicker, already up and running by the time I am on my feet, disappearing out of sight through the grove.

I round a line of trees and see Mari holding Kidlat to her.

"What is it?" I pant. "Not a snake?" I scan the ground around them.

"No," says Mari, and her voice is strange, mesmeric. "Ami, look up."

I crane my neck back. The branches are burning.

It is just like the orphanage fire—the trees flickering gold and red and brown—but there is no heat. I blink stupidly, trying to stop my mind tricking me, like it did with the rotten fruit, trying to see this for what it really is. Some of the flames resolve themselves into flowers, but the others shift and flutter like leaves, and it takes me a long moment to make shapes I recognize out of them. The branches are not covered in flames . . .

They're wings.

My mind flicks to *diwata*, but then Mari claps and they lift in a great swell, not fast and angry like the flies, but like birds, swooping as if through water.

"Mariposas," she says in the same, wondering voice.

And now I can see them clearly for what they are: the colors patterning each wing, the black bodies, some large, some small, and all of them shifting like breath across the clearing. Butterflies. Dozens, maybe hundreds of them, coasting on the air like a visible, fluttering wind. I wonder if Nanay and Ama's *gumamela* flowers had brought so many.

"I—" I want to say it's beautiful but the word feels silly and flimsy in my mouth. If beauty had a color, had a shape or a taste or a smell, it would be the color, shape, taste and smell of this moment. Exactly this.

Mari's hand slides into mine and we watch as the butterflies glide over our heads, twirling around the flowers and fruit, dipping so low I could reach out and brush their wings. Some hang in drips from branches, like oil thinking

187

of dropping off a spoon. In the lower branches, at eye height, are endless rows of chrysalises. Some are green, some brown, but most are transparent. Showing through some of them are wings, but most of them are empty, leaving only filmy, cylindrical twists.

I walk away, dropping Mari's hand. The trees, I realize now, are flame trees. Their flowers are red and splashed across the branches, showing through the coat of brown and yellow and blue. It is late for them to be flowering, so close to the rains. One miraculous thing follows another in this forest. A lump rises in my throat. Nanay loves butterflies and it's she who brought me through this forest to this fruit farm. I want to stand there forever, and it is beginning to feel as if we will when Mari breaks the whispering silence.

"Come on," she says, shaking off the trance. "We're so close. We shouldn't stop now."

I nod. The butterflies have lifted at her voice and are swirling again. They rise off the eddy of the air like leaves shedding water, wings shining.

We turn away slowly, my heart dropping with every step. But when we walk on through the trees, there are more, hanging from fruit and from each other, and taking flight as we walk past until a flock is beating its way above our heads. Anything else in this number would be frightening, but I am learning that it is impossible to be scared of butterflies.

We rejoin the river on the far side of the rotten mango grove, and again the road is visible from the bank. We are so close now. With our escort of wings above us, around us, we walk through the butterfly forest. Before I've noticed the time passing or the distance closing, we are in front of the small, rocky escarpment that marks the outer boundary of the town. The water slides beneath it, but we have to climb.

We crawl, keeping our bodies close to the rocks, and lie on our bellies to peer over the top. Buildings come into sight—the backs of houses and the low-slung shadow of a fence. There were never houses this close to the forest before. I'm not sure how we are going to get to the hospital without being noticed. I can hear Touched children laughing from the gardens ahead as the butterflies swoop around them. Culion is swarming with them. I hope Nanay has seen them.

I feel something light brush my face, and a large blue-and-white butterfly lands neatly on the back of my hand. It opens and closes its wings once, twice.

"Ami." Mari says my name slowly. "Don't move."

"I know," I breathe. "It's amazing."

"No." Her voice is tight, a coiled spring. "Don't. Move."

Then I feel something else. A weight on my leg, moving across my calves. Slithering. My body tenses.

"Don't move!" Mari breathes.

I try to remember what Nanay told me about snakes. *A hundred different kinds and only ten that are poisonous.* The weight is shifting up my thigh, and I try not to shudder as I feel it cross my lower back. My insides are locked in a silent scream. *They won't do harm unless you do harm, like* diwata. Up the flat of my

189

back now, and though it is impossible, I imagine I can feel the tongue flicking out across my back.

Mari has moved silently beside me to grab a large stone. I can see her hand from the corner of my eye, white-knuckled and shaking. *Only ten poisonous. More scared of you than you are of it.* The snake is nearing my shoulders. I wonder if I can move fast enough to flick it off before it has a chance to strike. I should have kicked it off my leg. I focus on the butterfly, its wings opening a third time, a fourth, the eye at the center of each shimmering on each beat.

The snake is over my shoulder, and it is all I can do to stop myself turning to look at it. I can see its head in my peripheral vision—a spadelike triangle. Through my panic comes a memory of a snake cornered in the kitchen, ready to strike. *A temple viper,* said Nanay, opening the back door wide and leading me out of the house. *Never anger it, best to leave it to find its own way out.* The tongue flicks. *Never anger it.*

Definitely poisonous. A chill descends my spine, although I am sweating in the heat. I can see Mari's hand clenching the stone tighter and suddenly the butterfly is lifting off my hand with a soft kiss of pressure and the snake strikes at it, fangs bared, piercing my skin.

A boiling brand burns down to my bones. And then Mari's stone comes smashing on top of it and Kidlat is screaming and just before I fade into the pain I think how Nanay always kissed me better if I hurt myself, and how everything is the wrong way round.

The End

Someone is saying my name. The voice is gentle but insistent. My eyelids feel heavy, gummed together. The ground under my back is soft, and I'm sinking into it like water.

"Ami, open your eyes now."

I don't want to, but the voice won't go away. I sigh deeply and tell my eyelids to lift. The slice of world is bright through my lashes, white and harsh. I close them again.

"No, Ami. You have to wake up." A hand grips my shoulder lightly and shakes. "It's time to wake up."

I know that voice. I know that voice is not Mari's, or Kidlat's. I open my eyes again, slowly. My tongue feels swollen and sticky.

"Sister Margaritte?" I say, though what actually comes out sounds quite different. Her face sharpens into focus after a few blinks.

"Hello, Ami."

I turn my head, and my neck aches. "Where?"

"The hospital. Culion Hospital. You've been here a few hours."

I'm alone in a room painted a bright white. The air is antiseptic and bitter. My right hand aches, and when I look down at it, all I can see is a thick mass of bandages. I hold my hand up and it throbs. "What—"

Sister Margaritte places it back on the pillow it was resting on. "I'm afraid your friend Mari did more damage than the snake. Someone heard them shouting for help, and thank goodness you were brought here quickly. Mari had killed and brought the snake, so we were able to give you the antivenin. Dr. Rodel set the wrist as best he could."

I can feel the pressure of a splint along my arm. "Is Mari all right?"

Sister Margaritte's face is serious suddenly. "Yes."

Something in her tone makes panic well up in me. "What?"

"She's gone, Ami. And Kidlat."

I blink stupidly. "Gone where?"

"Mr. Zamora took them." My heart sinks. "Tried to take you, too, but Dr. Rodel and Dr. Tomas insisted you were too unstable."

"Where did he take them?" I ask desperately. "Back to the orphanage?"

Her answer is exactly what I didn't want to hear.

"They've been relocated."

"To where? Manila?"

She shakes her head. "He didn't say."

"No!" We can't be separated, not after all this. I wanted her to meet Nanay, and to have someone to be with after ... after all this.

Sister Margaritte takes my good hand. "I know."

But she can't know. She can't know that Mr. Zamora has taken Mari to a fate she worked so hard to leave behind. To a workhouse. I blink up at Sister Margaritte. It is so strange to see her again, so strange to be back in Culion Town even though that is all I've wanted for weeks and weeks.

I throw off the covers, though the movement makes my hand twinge. "I'm not leaving."

"Yes, you are," says Sister Margaritte, taking my other wrist in a surprisingly strong grip. Something hits the window with a soft *thump*, and for one delicious moment I think it is Mari, dangling a message at the mesh to tell me she is waiting. But then another hits and I see it is a butterfly, throwing itself at the screen.

"Poor things," says Sister Margaritte sadly. "It's the light from the white walls, they seem drawn to it. You're lucky you have a screen, or the room would be full of them. They're every-where." Her eyes go distant. "It's quite beautiful, actually."

I pull on her sleeve. "Please, Sister. I've come all this way. You helped write Nanay's letters. You said I should come—"

193

"Yes, I am glad you are here. But you cannot *stay*, Ami." She says this sadly, and I can tell she is sorry to have to say it at all. "It is the way things are now."

"But I have to see Nanay—"

"Of course. Now you are here, you must." She stands, elegant in her black habit. "But no one must know, Ami. You understand?"

She reaches into her robes and pulls out a silver whistle. "This is to signal a fire. I am going to go outside and blow. When you hear it, go straight to room fourteen. It's just down the corridor, to the left. It takes ages to evacuate this place, and even longer to get back in. The rounds will be delayed, so you'll have a couple of hours at least—"

"A couple of hours!" I did not come so far for so little.

"Ami." Sister Margaritte's back is to me, but her voice cracks. I wait. She takes a deep breath and turns to me again. "Your *nanay*, she's—she's been waiting."

"I know, and that is exactly why an hour or two is not long enough—"

"No, Ami. She's been waiting to say goodbye. For her *pahimakas.*" Something spills down her cheek and I realize her eyes are bright with tears. It is like watching a statue weep.

I am so astonished by the tears I don't feel the words sink in until they are bubbling in my mind. *Waiting to say goodbye. Pahimakas.* Last farewell. She can't mean . . .

"No." The world is falling away. I can feel my face crumpling, and suddenly Sister Margaritte is sitting on the bed beside me;

her face is close to mine and she is holding my upper arms so tightly it hurts.

"No," she says quietly, fiercely. "Don't cry. Not yet." It is silly of her to say that when she is crying herself, but I make the tears stop on their way to my eyes.

"You made it, Ami," she says in that same blazing whisper. "You crossed the forest. You brought the butterflies. You survived the snakebite." She loosens her grip slightly, and her tone softens. "You are a remarkable girl. And your *nanay* needs you to be remarkable now. She's ready, but she's scared. I know that you are too, but you have time to be scared later. You can cry later. Give her hope, Ami. Give her courage."

I feel a heat welling inside me, the same fire I felt when Mr. Zamora was about to strike Mari on the clifftop. I will not let Nanay be afraid. I nod. Sister Margaritte stands up again and tilts her head back as if she's trying to make her tears flow backward.

"Good," she says in her normal voice. "Remember, left out of here. Room fourteen."

Then she is gone and I tell myself again and again to be remarkable. The whistle sounds outside my room and I hear her shout, "Corridor clear!" There are shouts and scuffling from somewhere farther away. I lower my legs out of bed, toes cramping slightly as my feet take my weight. My head spins and my hand thrums, but I make it to the door without stumbling. I listen at the keyhole for a moment before deciding the noises are all far away, then go out into the corridor.

This is painted a bright white too, and the paint has finger-prints in places where hands have touched the drying surface. The hospital never had a corridor before, or so many individual rooms. They have built so much, so fast. I turn left and pass rooms twelve, thirteen, stop outside fourteen. I want to take a breath, to ready myself, but there is no time to waste. I turn the handle and step inside.

The room is bare except for a wooden cross on the wall, a small table with a glass on it and a bed on which a small, huddled shape lies beneath thin white sheets. At the sound of the door closing, her head turns. I see it is swaddled in bandages. I hear her voice, and it is all I can do not to cry at the sound. She sounds very old, and tired.

"Ami?"

"Yes, Nanay."

I do not move closer. Despite what Sister Margaritte said, I am scared. Then Nanay maneuvers herself onto her side and I see her gentle eyes above the bandages and I forget the fear. I am only happy, happiness filling me head to toe as I cross to her side and bury my face in her neck. Through the bitter antiseptic she smells of her, earthy and sweet.

"Oh, Ami," she murmurs, holding me weakly. Her arms are not bandaged and her skin is smooth and warm through my hospital tunic. "You came."

"Of course I did."

"And what an adventure you've had."

"You've heard?" I say, disappointed.

She draws back and says, "Some of it, but I'd like to hear it from you."

She moves up in the narrow bed so I can climb in beside her, and I tell her. It is like one of our stories. I tell her about the orphanage and Sister Teresa, and butterfly lessons. She seems very tired and I wonder if she has been given the same thing Rosita was, a drug that makes you feel tired but painless and floating. I keep my mouth busy with my journey, remembering to be brave.

I tell her about the letters, and the fire, and *Lihim*. I tell her about the fish, and Kidlat. I tell her about walking and sleeping under the stars, Bondoc with the matches, the carpet of rotten fruit, and the snake. She holds my hand tightly at this part. But most of all I tell her about Mari, and the butterflies.

"That's a wonderful adventure, Ami. You'll remember that forever."

"Yes," I say.

"You sound sad . . . ?"

I am thinking of how quickly Mari will forget me. "The girl I came here with. She was taken away."

Nanay strokes my hand. "I'm sure you will find each other again. Sister Margaritte has sent for Bondoc. He's said he will look after you."

"What about Capuno?"

"Capuno is busy enough. He's teaching now, at the school here. You are the most precious thing, Ami. You will be looked after. You are loved." Her voice cracks and she looks away, through the window. "And the butterflies are miraculous, aren't they? Sister Margaritte says they're all over Culion, landing everywhere." Nanay sighs, her breath whistling worse than I have ever heard it. "I wish I could see them."

"There are so many, maybe even more than at your butterfly house."

"I'm sure." She smiles thinly. "Your *ama* loved them almost as much as me, and we both loved them for the same reason. Can you guess what it is?"

I think. "That they're beautiful?"

Nanay shakes her head, the movement making her wince. "Some butterflies only live a day, some a week, some a month. But they spend every one of those days busy living. And they make the world a more beautiful place, however brief their time."

Her arm tightens around me. She is saying these things as though she means something else by them. Her voice is sad and soft and I have to clench my jaw to keep from crying.

"I brought back your basin."

"You keep it. Ami, I—"

I don't want her to explain. I know already, from what she just said and from what Sister Margaritte told me. I think I knew even before that, from when I read the letter Mari stole

198

for me. But it doesn't make my chest hurt less, doesn't make it easier to breathe.

"Have you been going to church?" I say hurriedly, because I need to stop her from speaking and the cross is above us and it's all I can think of to say.

"Of course not." She reaches under her pillow and pulls out her terra-cotta gods. "But they've nailed that to the wall and won't take it down."

A butterfly flies with a *thump* at the window. A thought flits through my mind.

"They like the white. It's so sad," remarks Nanay. Then, "What are you doing?"

I wriggle out from under the covers, and cross to the window. The mesh is held in place in a wooden frame, wedged into the uneven square hole. I can tell it was done in a rush. I begin to press the wooden frame with my unsplinted hand.

"Ami, you'll get in trouble!" hisses Nanay, but she can't get out of bed to stop me. After a few moments the screen falls forward and out of sight.

As if it had been waiting, a single brown butterfly flies inside and lands on Nanay's white sheet. We are both silent for a few seconds, then Nanay laughs in delight and it is the first truly loud noise she's made. The butterfly takes off but it doesn't matter because more butterflies are coming in, drawn to the whiteness. By the time I have climbed back into bed beside Nanay, there are a dozen flitting around, landing on the sheets or the walls.

We watch them, Nanay holding my hand tight, as they fill the room like leaf-fall, swirling their invisible currents and weaving around our heads. Nanay kisses my forehead.

"Thank you, Ami."

"That's all right. Sister Margaritte says I brought the butterflies."

"And so you did." Nanay's voice is tired again. "Do you mind if I close my eyes for a while?"

There are so many things I want to say, but I'm scared if I speak, I'll cry, so I shake my head. We lie like we used to after I had a bad dream, Nanay's arm draped across me. She speaks softly into my hair. "It's all right, Ami. I'm not scared. I'm glad you came."

"I love you, Nanay."

"I love you," she says.

It feels almost good to cry. My body shakes and Nanay holds me to her until I can stop. I take deep breaths like she taught me as she begins telling me a jumble of stories, new ones and old ones and true ones, about the giants, and the house with flowers where she was happy with Ama, and butterfly forests. Her voice slows and dips; the butterflies swirl.

When she stops talking, I don't turn around. I hold my stomach tightly, as though squeezing will stop my insides from feeling like they're tearing apart. The room falls into a shadowy dusk, and then the door opens and Sister Margaritte is standing in a swarm of butterflies. Nanay's arm is heavy across me.

And still. The quiet of her no-breath is the loudest sound I have ever heard.

A giant, gentle hand moves Nanay's touch from my side. Bondoc lifts and folds me into his arms. There comes a silence so complete it can mean only one thing: outside, the sky cracks. Finally, the monsoon washes the air clean.

THIRTY YEARS LATER

One

Sol was lost. She had missed, somehow, the road back to Manila, and now was not sure she'd even remember the way back to the fruit farm. Her basket of oranges sat heavy as a brick on her head. She longed to take one from its twist of paper, to sink her thumbnail into the thick peel and pierce the flesh, suck it dry. Her mouth watered and she took a deep breath. She must resist. Cook, the maid and all of the orphans, herself included, had put their allowance aside for weeks to pay for these as a special treat for the mistress's birthday. They would never forgive her if she ate one.

Annoyance swelled briefly inside her. Why could Cook not have decided upon local oranges that filled the trees in the garden, and were so plentiful and cheap at market you could buy them by the barrel? Why did she insist that Mistress must have *these* oranges? They did not seem any different from market oranges, but from the way the farmer picked them from the tree and wrapped them individually in thin sheets of paper, you'd think they were made of glass. And why—and this was what made her fists clench and jaw tighten—was it *her,* only just thirteen and with a notoriously bad sense of direction, who had to make the two-hour-long journey on foot, along a route no bus took, and get so lost on the way back that soon the moon would be out?

She took another steadying breath. She knew Cook had meant no harm. It was a nice idea, and one that would make Mistress very happy. Sol softened. Things had been so much better since Mistress and her brother had taken over the orphanage five years ago. If anyone was deserving of a treat for their birthday, it was her. And now that Sol thought about it, she *had* volunteered in order to avoid helping out on laundry day. But still ... she shuddered.

These were not friendly forests. They were wild and untamed, a world away from the cultivated paddy fields that skirted Manila, miles from here. The day was shedding its light faster now, in that careless, urgent way that meant the sun was dropping toward the horizon.

She stopped for a moment, panting. It was not just the heat and the weight of the basket, but the beginnings of panic. She should go back, try to find the paths back to the farm. She closed her eyes, trying to remember which route she had taken.

Right, left, left, middle. No, that wasn't it. Right, left, middle, left. Oh, come on! Remember!

She opened her eyes again. It was no use. Her best hope was to keep following the faint path ahead. She stumbled on and suddenly reached the tree line. Ahead, the path mounted over a narrow ridge, pressed up like pastry edging a pie. It looked as crumbly, too, and she was careful not to get too close to the edge as she peered over.

Her heart sank. Below was a valley dark with more trees. A thick patch of red and blue flowers twisted across the center, and a thin river glinted like a silver blade through the forest, but there was no sign of a town, nor of a farm.

She placed the basket on the ground and slumped down beside it, kicking off her shoes and rubbing her aching feet. She looked at the paper-wrapped oranges. No harm now. She'd be in trouble for missing her shift in the kitchen when she got back anyway. *If* she got back.

She took a twist and unwrapped it, bringing the orange up to her nose and inhaling the scent. Her mouth watered as she stuck her thumb deep into the peel and pulled until the fruit sat round and perfect in her palm. She meant to eat it slowly, in segments, but her thirst took over and soon she had eaten it like an apple, the juice sticking her fingers together.

It was the most delicious thing she had ever tasted, far sweeter than the local market oranges. She lay back and stretched her arms over her head.

Soon the sun would set, leaving only a film of purple on the horizon. Above her, the half-moon hung pale as a ghost behind the last light of the day. A sense of calm came over her as she watched the moon growing brighter and the light smattering of stars scraping the edges of the still-light sky.

Something began to swoop and dive across her vision, coming so low she giggled with nerves, remembering Cook's story about the girl who had to cut off all her hair after a bat got tangled in it.

But it was not a bat.

Sol blinked. There were just one or two to begin with, but as she sat up, she realized the air was full of them. She rubbed her eyes.

Butterflies swirled like air currents up and over the ridge before her, as if magnetized. They were as plentiful as the fruit flies that rose at the hottest part of the day, and all seemed to be heading in the same direction. She crawled forward on her hands and knees, peering over the edge.

Smoke was rising in a steady column from the center of the patch of flowers in the forest below. It was no forest fire. It was a chimney. And the butterflies were swarming toward it.

Sol was up and over the crumbling ridge before she could think twice. The butterflies flitted overhead as she let gravity pull her down, skidding on her heels and gripping roots wherever she could. Her bare feet stung as the blisters opened.

Once she came level with the tree line, the smoke was obscured from her view, but it did not matter. The butterflies were still snaking through the trees around her. Catching her breath at the base of the slope, she stretched out her arms and they flooded around her fingers, so close she fancied she could feel the kiss of the air pushed by their wings brushing her hands. One alighted on her upturned thumb, an iridescent blue in the dusk, with veins of black shot through the shimmer. She watched it open and close its wings once, twice, then rejoin the swarm.

Sol felt giddy. She stumbled, crouching to wait for the faintness to pass, and when she looked up again, the stream of butterflies had petered out.

In panic she ran forward, catching sight of the last of them as they whipped around a corner like a tail. She followed them into a sudden clearing, the trees felled and the grass tramped down. At the center of the clearing was a huge tumble of red flowers, on a bush as big as a house. Sol looked closer.

It *was* a house. The walls were wreathed in flowers, and there was the smoke she had seen, rising from the center of the roof. Except now that she was nearby, it did not smell like ordinary smoke. It was scented like honey, mixing with the sweetness of the flowers. The butterflies danced around the column, and she noticed they were flying clumsily now, butting up against each other, dipping down, then lurching up again.

Her heart began to beat even faster. This was not right. Something in the smoke—something was hurting them.

Sol stepped forward. She wanted to swat them away from the smoke, but the roof was too high.

Then they began falling, like ash. Most landed on the

flowered roof and walls, but some came down before her, landing at her feet like jeweled leaves.

"No!" She knelt carefully and tried to lift one, but its wings
turned to powder between her shaking fingers. She tried again
with another as a bright light lit up one of the flowered walls.
A door, opening.

"Stop!"

Two

Sol's heart pounded. She dropped her hands to her sides and squinted at the figure in the doorway.

"Don't touch them!" The voice spoke again, urgently. "Stay very still."

She did as she was told, sinking back on her heels. The figure was silhouetted against the light: a square shape that could have been a man or a woman, young or old. Sol's fingertips were sticky with the juice of the orange, covered in dust and the bright colors of butterfly wings. She began to cry.

"It's all right, child," said the voice, kinder and closer now. "I know you didn't mean any harm."

She looked up through a kaleidoscope of tears, and saw it was a woman, using a stretched piece of net to lift the prone butterflies onto the flowers. Except now that she looked closely, they were not dead at all. Their wings were opening and closing, so the house rippled like water. She made to stand but the woman spoke again, softly.

"Just stay there a minute longer, I'm nearly done. How many did you touch?"

"T-two," she said. "I'm so sorry, I thought they were hurt."

"Only dazed," said the woman as she lifted the injured butterflies onto her palm. She clenched her jaw, then brought her other hand down hard on the bodies. Sol flinched at the sound.

"It's kinder that way. They can't survive without their wings," said the woman as she scanned the ground carefully.

"Why are they all asleep?"

"It's the smoke. I put herbs in it, and it brings them home to rest. It's not safe at night, what with the bats and snakes."

Sol did not know what to say to this, and watched as the woman carefully maneuvered a final black-and-red butterfly onto a flower, then leaned the net against the wall.

"And besides," the woman continued, walking toward her. "Never touch a butterfly on its wings, hurt or otherwise. You'll only hurt it more. They're too delicate for human touch."

Sol nodded, and stood up as the woman approached. She had an open, kind face with big, dark eyes. Close up, she looked about Mistress's age.

"So," said the woman. "Now you know not to touch a butterfly, but you should know already not to wander in the forests alone and so close to dark."

It took Sol a couple of seconds to realize that the woman wanted an explanation. Her brain was still filled with butterflies.

"I got lost."

"I guessed that." The woman smiled. "Where were you heading?"

"Manila."

"Ah. You are very lost indeed." She turned back to her house. "You had better stay here tonight."

"I can't! My mistress—"

"Wouldn't want you unsafe, I am sure. I'm going to Manila tomorrow anyway, to give a talk at a school. I can give you a lift."

Sol looked behind her at the darkly swaying forest, and her resolve crumbled. She followed the woman toward the lit slice of door. The house was big inside, with paper partitions on runners pushed back against the walls to make one large room, the scented fire at the center.

"Are you hungry? I have some rice, or oranges."

Sol slapped a hand to her forehead. "Oh, no!"

"What is it?"

"I left the oranges up there," said Sol, pointing out of the open door. "My shoes, too."

"What oranges?"

"The ones I bought from the farm over the hill. They're a gift, for my mistress. Nearly thirty of them."

The woman wrinkled her nose. "Do they not have oranges in Manila?"

"Cook said they're not as fine as these," said Sol, unable to keep the edge out of her voice.

"That's true enough." Her voice was warm and calming, like sweet tea. "I own those orange groves, and I do agree that they are special. It's a variety that only grows in a few places in the world."

She stood and walked to a shadowy corner, lifting a crate from beneath a table. "Here, you can take these."

Sol peered in. It was full of oranges the same size as the ones she had left. "But I can't pay for them—"

"No need." The woman waved her hand. "They're a gift."

"Thank you," said Sol, relief flooding through her. "But I have to get my shoes from the hill anyway—"

"You can't go now. It's too dark. You can fetch them tomorrow, before we leave for Manila."

Sol did not want to argue. The house was comfortably cool and bright, and the woman was holding out a cup of tea to her. "Drink up."

It was as warm and sweet as her voice. Sol finished it in four deep gulps, setting the tea leaves swirling. The woman stood to refill the cup from a kettle over the fire. Sol looked around. The floor consisted of a thick mat of plaited dried grass, and the few pieces of furniture were square and sturdy, like the woman.

"It's not much," said the woman. "But it's home."

"It's lovely!"

It was. It felt as though the house had been there as long

as the forest, sprouting chairs and windows like roots and branches.

The woman's face broke into a wide smile. "I think so. But there are far grander houses in the city."

"Where I live, the floors have carpets, so it's always hot. And the people aren't so grand as their houses would have you believe."

The woman frowned, the lines splitting her face making her look far older than she had the moment before. "I hope your mistress is not cruel to you?"

"Oh, she's very kind, and I'm not her servant. She runs the orphanage. I'm—" Sol hesitated. She hated the pity that always followed the next words. "An orphan."

"Me too," said the woman, a sad smile on her face. They sat quietly a moment, the teacup cooling between Sol's palms.

"Anyway," the woman said, clucking her tongue. "It's a strange world where someone may run an orphanage with carpets, and yet not even think to give the orphans shoes."

Sol remembered her bare feet. "Oh, I have shoes! I left them with the oranges."

"Ah, yes, you did tell me." The woman rapped her forehead suddenly, as if she were knocking on a door. "Silly me! And I haven't even asked your name. I do things all out of order, you'll soon see. What is your name?"

"Sol."

"Lovely. And I am Amihan." She paused and cleared her throat before asking, "Do you like it at the orphanage, Sol?"

Sol shrugged. "It's all right. It used to be horrible, but since Mistress took over, it's been quite nice." *Almost like a home,* she thought, but she had had enough of talking about herself, her small and boring life with its small and boring details. The words that had been burning her tongue forced their way out before she could stop them, coming out high and garbled: "The butterflies!"

Amihan looked at her over the rim of her cup.

"The butterflies," Sol tried again. "What—why are they here?"

Amihan swallowed. "They are here because I am here."

"Are they yours?"

"Not truly," the woman said. "But I care for them. I am more theirs than they are mine."

Sol frowned. "Do you feed them?"

"I planted the flowers they feed on. I look after them at night, put out nets to stop the bats. In return, they let me study them."

Sol had a sudden flash of inspiration. "Like a butterfly collector?"

The woman's open face seemed to snap shut and darken, her eyes suddenly fierce. "No, nothing like a butterfly collector." She spat out the words. "I do not need to kill beautiful things to understand them. I do not need to trap a wild thing to hang on my wall like a painting."

Sol's mouth went dry. "I'm sorry, I—"

"No," interrupted the woman, the clouds rolling back. "I'm sorry. I— It's a common mistake. In truth, there is no word for what I am. Some call others in my line of work lepidopterists, or aurelians."

"What's an aurelian?" The word felt graceful on Sol's clumsy tongue. It was fine and shining, like golden lace.

The woman smiled at the confusion on Sol's face. "Just a fancy word for a butterfly collector, only with more science. But other aurelians kill the butterflies to study them. I do not. I create living museums for gardens."

"How?"

"I plant the flowers they like, and sometimes I make netting or glass enclosures to keep them safe and warm."

"Like a butterfly zookeeper?"

The woman clapped her hands together happily. One of them was lumpy with scar tissue, and Sol tried not to stare. "Yes! Exactly that. I shall have to get my sign redone."

She jerked her head to the door and Sol noticed a rectangular piece of wood hanging there. It was painted a rich blue, with careful gold letters.

AMIHAN TALA
AURELIAN
Butterfly Gardens a Speciality
Inquiries Welcome

"I hang it by the main road when the festival trade passes. Mostly people just come to ask me what it means, but I get enough work. And what do you do?"

217

Sol frowned. "I'm a child. I go to school and do chores—"

Amihan brushed this response aside. "No, no. What do you do?"

"I help Cook—"

"No!" said the woman, firmly but not unkindly. "What are you good at? What do you like doing? What are you going to do for the rest of your life?"

Sol thought hard, wanting to come up with an answer that would please her. A teacher? A secretary? These were perhaps a little ambitious. But yet here was this woman in the middle of the forest, living in a house covered in butterflies. It made impossible things feel a little more possible. "A butterfly zookeeper."

"That," said Amihan, leaning forward with a solemn expression, "is a very good idea indeed."

Sol felt warmth blossom inside her. "How did you become one?"

"Ah," said the woman, "to understand that, I'd have to begin at the beginning. It is a very long story. And therefore, possibly very boring."

"I don't see how it can be," said Sol.

"Aren't you tired?"

Sol shook her head firmly. "Not at all."

She wasn't. The air had taken on an almost electrical charge. The thrill of it ran across the hairs of her arms.

"Tell me," said the woman, leaning back in her chair. "Have you heard of Culion?"

"The leper colony?"

"Mmm." Sol could feel the woman's eyes on her as she spoke. "What do you know about it?"

"That it is full of lepers." Sol tried not to shudder. Her eyes flicked to the woman's scarred hand.

The woman laughed dryly. "That is true enough. And what do you think about that?"

"Not much," said Sol.

"Not much?"

"It is not a nice thing to think about."

"Why? Because it scares you?"

"Because it's disgusting!"

It was the woman's turn to flinch.

"In my experience," Amihan said, "disgust is the consequence of fear. Why are you afraid of lepers, Sol?"

Sol shuddered and thought of the old man who sometimes came begging for alms at the door. Mistress always made them invite him in and give him food, and once Sol had answered the door and his fingerless hand had brushed hers. But it seemed a silly answer to give. All the children were afraid of him, and said far worse things than Sol had. It was just how it was.

But she could tell she had angered Amihan. The atmosphere between them had changed again. It was like being in the room with a cloud: one moment the woman was soft and pillowy, the next gray and threatening storms.

"I meant—"

"I know what you meant." Amihan was far away now, eyes fixed on the wall above Sol's head. "And I have to tell you that kindness is an important part of being a butterfly zookeeper. Do you think what you said was kind?"

"No," said Sol, her own voice hushed to match the woman's.

There was a long silence. Amihan's expression was inscrutable, a mist on a windless day. Sol squirmed.

"I'm sorry," she said eventually. "I was unkind."

"I am only sorry you feel disgusted by people who are different. People who are suffering, and who do you no harm other than existing."

It was as bad as if Amihan had shouted, and Sol hurried to move the conversation on. "Is that how you became an aura—an aralan?"

"Aurelian."

"Aurelian." Again Sol let the word drift out, like a shimmering breeze. "By being kind?"

"No," said the woman, her eyes like coals burning with the last of the fire's light. "I got here by luck. And love, of course. That is behind most stories, long or short. Behind most journeys, too. And it was a big journey that brought me here."

"You weren't born here?"

The woman shook her head.

"Where were you born, then?"

The woman looked at her, mock-serious. "Can't you guess?"

"Culion?" Sol gaped at her. "But . . . but how did you leave?"

"Again—by luck, and love. By having them, and losing them again."

Three

The woman's voice was low, mesmeric, peppered with pauses when she'd look around the room as if casting about for the next part of her story. And as it went on, from a childhood spent with lepers, to an orphanage, and a friendship with a girl named for butterflies, and a crossing made on an abandoned boat, Sol should have become more sure that this was what it was: a story that Amihan was conjuring from the darkness.

But Sol knew, sure as the nighttime silence, that it was true, that when Amihan stopped talking, it was only to relive the words, to remember what she saw. And when she reached the butterfly swarm, Sol closed her eyes, remembering chasing the wings down the hillside. Her eyes ached and did not want to open, but she did not want to miss a word.

The longest pause stretched between Amihan telling of Nanay's silence, the touch of Bondoc's hand, and the coming of the monsoon. Sol looked up sharply.

"Your *nanay* didn't *die*?" she asked, shocked. She could feel tears running down her cheeks but she didn't care. She had thought there would be a happier ending to the story.

The woman nodded slowly. "I'm afraid she did."

"But that's not fair!"

"That," said the woman, "is not entirely true."

Sol stared at her uncomprehendingly.

"It is sad," said the woman. "It broke my heart. But she was very sick. She was in pain. It took me years to realize it, but it was kinder that way."

"Like Mari said?" said Sol, keen to show she had been paying attention.

The woman's voice went small and soft. "Yes, like Mari said."

"Did you find her? Or Kidlat?"

"I looked for as long as I could stand the heartache. I went to every workhouse and orphanage I could find, but they were not in Manila, or any of the other big cities or towns. He must have taken them elsewhere. There was no trace of them."

Sol could tell the woman didn't want to talk more about Mari, so she searched rapidly for another question. "And all that happened to *you*?"

Sol could not quite reconcile this woman with the young

girl she had once been. It is always hard to imagine adults having childhoods.

The woman laughed. "Other people's pasts seem like another country, don't they? Telling you made it strange for me, too. Though it is my own story."

"What happened to the butterflies?"

"The monsoon happened," Amihan said simply. "The next day the streets were awash with dead butterflies." Her expression softened slightly at Sol's stricken face. "It's not a very happy part of the story, is it?"

Sol shook her head, her jaw tight.

"But it was incredible they came at all. That those few samples dropped by Mr. Zamora grew into a swarm."

"I wish it could have been a happier ending," mumbled Sol.

"But it is a happy ending." Amihan gestured around them. "Look where I ended up."

"Why here?" said Sol.

"Don't you recognize it?" asked Amihan kindly. "A house covered in flowers?"

Sol gasped. "You didn't—you didn't *find* him? Your father?"

Another sad smile flickered on Amihan's face. "No. I was too late for that. But I found the house. As soon as Bondoc and I arrived in Manila, we asked every person we knew, and many we didn't, whether they had heard of a blue-roofed house in a valley, covered in red flowers. One day I asked a woman selling tea in the market and she told me she once passed such a house, a few miles from Manila."

"I thought your father was a leper—sorry—Touched." Sol paused, hoping she had remembered this detail correctly among the flood of this woman's life. "I thought all the Touched were brought to Culion?"

"Well, the only people who knew he was there—*here*—were either dead or ignorant of the fact he was Touched. No one was going to bother a man living in the middle of nowhere. Except me, of course."

She grinned and Sol saw a flash of the Amihan from the story—youthful, amazed and delighted by the way the world worked.

"So I bought some tea as a gift, and walked to see him. But the house was more forest than house. His illness had worsened shortly after Nanay was taken from him. I was years late. He had died at home and was buried in a grove nearby by some locals. His grave was overgrown when I arrived, vines growing up the wooden stake they used to mark it." She paused and swallowed hard. "I left it like that so the butterflies would visit him. But Bondoc helped me fix up the house and I suppose it is wrong to say I did not find a father here. Bondoc grew into a fine one. We had some very happy years together."

"Did Bondoc adopt you?"

"No, nothing so official!" Amihan laughed. "But he loved me like a daughter, and he had loved Nanay like a wife. It was the greatest sorrow of his life that he never got to say goodbye to her. At least I had that, though it took me many years to feel grateful for it."

"But he had you," said Sol quickly, not wanting to return to the sadness. "And you were happy."

"Of course I was," said Amihan. "I am. How can I not be, in a place like this? And I planted a grove full of Mari's favorite oranges to keep part of her close by. If you have or make something someone loves, I believe it brings them to you, even if they are not there."

"Like your *nanay*'s basin under your pillow?"

"Exactly."

"Is the butterfly swarm why you decided to be a butterfly zookeeper?"

"It was not so much a decision as a happening."

Sol waited until the woman explained.

"Well, this house has always attracted them, and a couple of years after Bondoc died, I was bored with selling herbs. A scientist who'd heard about the 'butterfly house' came and photographed it."

She pointed to a framed black-and-white print hanging above the door.

"He said he was a lepidopterist and would I be interested in selling him some butterflies."

"Did you give him the butterflies?"

Amihan shook her head. "He wouldn't agree to keep them alive. But he gave my name to some other scientists in Asia, and I was asked to create butterfly zoos for them. Once, I even traveled to a place called London, in England, and talked about my techniques."

"You've been to England?" Sol had never met anyone who'd left the Philippines, let alone crossed oceans.

"Yes. I gave a lecture at one of their societies." She pointed to another framed photo on the opposite wall: a grainy picture of her standing at a podium. "But that is another story."

"What was it like?"

"Cold."

Sol nodded. She had heard this from Cook, who read books set there. "Do you still travel?"

Amihan stretched. "Not so much now. I like it here. I mostly make zoos for wealthy local families now." She grimaced slightly. "Less science, more art."

Sol hesitated before asking her next question. She did not want to pull Amihan back into the dark places of her past, but longed to know one last thing.

"What happened to . . . to—"

"Mr. Zamora?" Amihan pointed to her bookshelf. "Second row, eighth one along."

Sol pushed her tired body to its feet and found the book. The spine was a rich red, with gold lettering stamped along it: *Butterfly Lives* by Dr. N. Zamora. She gaped and pulled it out, holding it warily.

"He finished his book?"

Amihan nodded. "And many more besides, but I only

226

bought the one he wrote at the orphanage. I didn't want to fill his pockets."

"Why did you buy this one?" Sol wrinkled her nose at the handsome tome.

"Because it's good," said Amihan simply. "It taught me a lot. And if I can take one good thing from my encounter with him, it's better than only bad things."

Sol bristled. "He should be in prison."

The woman chuckled. "I seem to remember someone having not dissimilar views only a few hours ago." Sol's face flushed, but Amihan's expression was kindly. "And besides, he's years dead. By all accounts he lived in a prison of his own making by the end. His sickness got worse and worse—it was punishment enough, I think."

Sol frowned. "You sound almost sorry for him."

"I am *very* sorry for him." Amihan's face was in shadow. "He did not have a life even a quarter as good as mine has already been."

There fell a great, deep silence that yawned almost as widely as Sol did. Amihan smiled. "You should get some rest—we have to get going in a few hours."

She settled Sol in her low bed, and took the chair by the fire for herself. It did not take long for Sol to fall into a sleep that swirled and shone with butterflies.

Four

Sol woke to the smell of frying. She sat up, rubbing her eyes, amazed that the butterfly house was not a dream. The butterfly zookeeper looked around and smiled. "Eggs or fruit?"

"Eggs, please. Is that it?"

"Is what it?"

"The basin, your *nanay*'s basin!"

Amihan looked down at the eggs. "Well remembered. You know, I never did get the garlic taste out of it."

They took their breakfast outside and ate their faintly garlicky omelets, watching the butterflies begin to take flight. The house was even more beautiful in the sunrise, the pale light making the red flowers brighter, the butterflies glowing like extra petals over them.

When she'd finished, Amihan said, "We should get going. I can't be late for my talk at the school. I just need to put on my work clothes."

She disappeared inside and emerged a few minutes later in a man's suit, complete with waistcoat and silver fob watch. Sol stared.

"Like it?" asked Amihan, taking a bowler hat from a hook by the door and tilting it on her head. "I bought it in London. It's made for London weather, so I do get a bit warm in it, but I love the shock it gives people."

Sol had never seen a woman in a suit before, but Amihan did look marvelous.

Sol watched as she caught a drowsy blue butterfly in a glass dome with a wooden base. "Is that a killing jar? Like Mr. Zamora had?"

"I've given it a new purpose." Amihan smiled. Beneath the base she placed another wooden dish, with a hollow in which a smoldering herb could be placed. "It's a resting jar now. It'll keep the butterfly calm. I need to take one to show at the school. This kind's rare. It'd be better if they would come here, but you know city folk. They always think their time is more important than anyone else's."

Sol followed the besuited woman out of the butterfly house to a stable housing a squat mule. "This is Siddy," Amihan said, patting the animal's neck. "Because he's forever trying to spirit me off on adventures."

As Amihan readied the mule and cart, Sol ran to collect her shoes. She climbed the hill, calves straining, but at the top she found only the basket coated in orange mush, a few fragments of leather and the buckles from her sandals. They'd been eaten beyond recognition. Scanning the ground around her, Sol saw a busy line of ants bearing away some orange peel. She should've known better than to leave food in the forest.

She arrived back at the house nearly in tears. "The ants . . ."

"Ah," said Amihan. "I should've seen that coming."

"What am I going to do? I can't go back without shoes. Mistress only bought them a couple of months ago."

"Nonsense, you can have a pair of mine." Amihan bustled inside and brought out a pair of brown leather shoes, worn soft and only slightly too big.

She hugged Sol, who was suddenly feeling very tired and tearful.

"Don't cry. This is my fault, keeping you awake so late with that silly story when all you needed was a good night's sl—"

"It wasn't silly!" said Sol indignantly. "I'm glad you told me. I'm glad I met you, even though my sandals got eaten."

"I'm glad I met you, too." Amihan released her gently. "I've had a thought."

"What kind of thought?"

"A good one." Amihan's eyes twinkled. "But I can't tell you yet."

"Why not?"

Amihan tapped the side of her nose. Sol looked at her, confused. Amihan repeated the gesture and said, "That means it's a secret, but all will be revealed." Sol copied her and Amihan laughed. "Exactly. We really do need to leave, though. Especially as I need to talk to your mistress first."

They climbed into the cart, and Sol twisted around in her seat so she could watch the house fade from view through the trees. As soon as it was gone, she might have felt that it had never existed at all, but for the crate of replacement oranges at her feet, the suit-clad woman beside her and the jewel-bright butterfly on her lap.

The road they took through the forest was so winding Sol was sure she'd never have found it on her own. Being in the butterfly house was like going back in time, and now, as the forest thinned and their road joined a paved, busy thoroughfare, it was as if the clock had been wound forward at double speed.

By the time they reached Manila, the streets were already packed. Some people turned to stare at Amihan in her suit and bowler, but the woman only smiled and doffed the hat at them. Sol supposed she was used to people staring. She began to direct Amihan through the twisting streets to her mistress's house.

"This is it." Sol indicated where to stop the cart. Amihan looked up at the gleaming sign.

HOPE CHILDREN'S HOME
20 THE AVENUE
MANILA
PROPRIETORS: MR. & MISS REY

"I need to go around the back," continued Sol, "so Cook doesn't see me. I'll be in trouble."

Amihan clucked her tongue. "Ridiculous. You shall come in the front with me."

She tucked the glass dome under one arm, and took Sol's hand in hers. "Ring the doorbell, please."

Sol, emboldened by Amihan's confidence, did so.

Cook opened the door with a wooden spoon in her hand, looking harried. The sound of a baby crying rose toward them. Cook's face froze in a caricature of shock as she took in the woman's bowler hat, the butterfly and Sol at her side, dusty and grinning.

"Hello there," said Amihan jovially. "I'm Amihan, living lepidopterist and butterfly zookeeper." She squeezed Sol's hand at this. "Sol found my house last night. She got lost on the way back from the orange farm, I believe. And if you don't mind me saying so, it's a bit careless of you to allow her to make such a journey alone."

"I..." Cook's eyes flicked from Sol to Amihan to her bowler hat.

"In fact, I should rather like to speak to you about Sol's future. She's a bright young girl, and I believe she has all the makings of a butterfly zookeeper."

232

"I . . ."

"Please, let me finish. I should very much like to discuss the possibility of apprenticing her."

"I . . ." Cook was braced against the doorframe, her wooden spoon held up against the barrage of Amihan's words, dripping gravy.

Hot sparks somersaulted inside Sol's stomach. "You can't mean—"

Amihan looked down at her with her warm brown eyes. "I very much do mean." She turned her attention back to Cook. "Well?"

Sol could barely speak through her grin. "That's Cook."

"Oh, I apologize, I thought you were the mistress," said Amihan, bowing deeply. Cook giggled, wiping her hands down her grease-stained apron. "Could I have a word with her before I go to my talk?"

"Of course," said Cook, seeming to remember herself. "Come in, please."

Amihan dropped her hand as they stepped inside and instantly Sol felt a little less brave.

"I'll just go and fetch her. Sol, can you—"

"Sol stays here," said Amihan, an edge of sharpness in her voice.

Cook gestured for them to follow her into the front sitting room. "Wait here."

Sol felt especially grubby in the pristine room, which Mistress kept for entertaining rich women who came to coo and donate money to their cause. Amihan settled in a carved wooden armchair with silk cushions, crossing her legs like a man and looking as comfortable as if she lived there, not in a wild house covered in wings. After a few moments Cook returned alone.

"She won't come," she said apologetically. "She's busy with the baby. Got left on the doorstep two nights ago, poor thing, and won't stop fretting."

"Then I shall have to go to her," said Amihan, up on her feet and striding past Cook before she could react. Sol scuttled after her, Cook just behind, as they followed the baby's cries down the hall. Amihan stopped outside the day nursery door and raised her hand to knock, but froze. Her dark face paled.

"What is it?" whispered Cook to Sol, but Sol shook her head.

Amihan lifted a finger to her lips. It seemed as if she was holding her breath. Beneath the baby's sobs the mistress's voice was just audible, singing low and soft.

"Listen!" Amihan hissed. Sol listened. It was Spanish, and she didn't understand the words. Then Amihan started singing along in Tagalog.

> Find me a boat and we'll float to the sea,
> Come, little one, come, there is so much to be.
> The world is so big and there's so much to see,
> Come, little one, come and go floating with me.

The crying inside dipped and the singing stopped.

"Who's there?" asked a voice sharply.

234

There were brisk footsteps, and as the door opened, Sol stumbled instinctively backward.

The master stood in the doorway. At the sight of Amihan his face drained of color. They looked at each other, and around them formed a silence so complete and so deep Sol felt she could fall into it.

"Well?" said the mistress's voice. "Who is it, Kidlat?"

A string yanked at Sol's insides. She had never heard Mr. Rey's first name, and until this moment had never cared. But now it all revealed itself, sure and bright as daylight.

Mr. Rey shrank back into the room, and a moment later the mistress appeared in the doorway, the quieting baby on her hip, light hair disheveled. From behind Amihan, Sol saw her pale eyes widen as her expression shifted into disbelief. She held a gloved hand up to her mouth.

The two women looked at each other, the clock ticking into the stilled moment. Then Mistress gently passed the baby to Mr. Rey, who took her, cooing softly. Finally, Amihan slid the mistress's glove off her hand, and Sol saw that it was small and nubbed.

"Hello, Mari," said the butterfly zookeeper.

Sol saw what would follow, with the shining clearness of a sky after rain: the life Mari had talked about one night on Culion Island, all those years ago. *Somewhere with trees and flowers and fruit and a river.* A house with Amihan, in the heart of a forest, its walls alive and blazing with butterflies.

Author's Note

Fiction is sometimes at its best when there is fact at its heart. Culion Island is a real place in the Philippines, and it really did become the world's largest leper colony between 1906 and 1998. (I use the word "leper" begrudgingly, as it is considered taboo by many people I spoke to who have lived in such colonies.)

Leprosy was widespread for millennia throughout Asia, Africa and Europe until a cure was developed and made internationally available in the 1980s. Cases still number in the hundreds of thousands, but many of these are cured. It is a hugely stigmatizing condition, linked to dirtiness and sin when in fact it is simply a bacteriological disease. It is very hard to catch, and cannot be transmitted by touch.

From 1906 to 1910 alone, 5,303 men, women and children

were transported to Culion Island. People's lives were torn apart by this forced migration—each of those individuals had a life, a family. Someone who would miss them. And so I decided to write a story that would put the reader at the center of the experience, through the eyes of Ami, a girl who is taken from her mother, and wants to find her way home.

Stories are often better if you tilt the truth enough to let some imagination seep in, and so I have taken liberties with the timeline of events, names and sometimes even geography. But I have stayed true to the people and place, and have tried to show that they are never only one thing: bad people can make beautiful things; good people can make grave mistakes.

The people who came up with the idea to turn Culion into a colony weren't evil—but they did see the inhabitants of the island as lepers before they saw them as human beings. When you reduce people to one trait—be it race, religion, whom they love—and don't step back to see the whole person, it is too easy to treat them as less than human.

You can still visit Culion Island. You can see the eagle, the church, the hospital, though the patients are long gone. It may have been known as the island of the living dead, the island of no return, or, as I have chosen to call it, the island at the end of everything. But for me, and for Ami, it was the start of everything, too.

Acknowledgments

To my family, who brought me kind words and nourishment as I sat at my grandparents' table in Norfolk, frantically typing this, my second story, while the rejections for my first pinged into my inbox. Thank you for not batting an eyelid as I maniacally grinned and explained over dinner that its major themes were "leprosy and butterflies." Thanks especially to my mum, Andrea, who read at least five drafts and resisted teasing me too much about my spelling.

To my friends and family around the world who bought outrageous numbers of *The Girl of Ink & Stars*, and asked when the next one was out. I'm deeply grateful. I hope you enjoyed it—especially you, Sabine!

To my beta and sensitivity readers: Andrea Millwood

Hargrave, the Unruly Writers, Sarvat Hasin, Daisy Johnson, Joe Brady, Janis Cauthery, Tom de Freston, Claire Donnelly, Hazel at staybookish.net and Louise Gornall.

To the online and in-life book community who have championed me and my first book, and encouraged me with my second: Malorie Blackman, Fiona Noble, Abi Elphinstone, Claire Legrand, Lucy Lapinski, Emma Carroll, Lucy Saxon, Carrie Hope Fletcher, Anna James, Katherine Webber, Pie Corbett, Mathew Tobin, Steph Elliot, Stevie Finegan, Sally the Dark Dictator, Mariyam Khan, Mariam Khan and so many more besides (you know who you are!). To my readers, and to the booksellers who made last year the best of my life, despite Brexit, etc., especially James, Rebecca, Alex and Paul at Blackwells, Zoe, Dani and Rachel at Waterstones Oxford and Florentyna.

To Melinda Salisbury, who took me to see the butterflies.

To Chicken House and all who sail in her: Elinor, Kesia, Esther, Laura M., Laura S., Jazz, Rachel H. and my editors Barry Cunningham and Rachel Leyshon. To Rachel Hickman and Helen Crawford-White for yet another stunning design. To my fellow Chickens: M. G. Leonard, Maz Evans, Lucy Strange, James Nicol, Ally Sherrick, Natasha Farrant, Sophia Bennett, Louise Gornall and Catherine Doyle—your books provide such escape, joy and inspiration.

To Maya and Mary Alice, partners in crime (and wine).

To Oscar, Noodle and Luna. I've not completely lost it—I know cats can't read (right?)—but this book could not have been written without one or another of you purring on my lap.

To Sarvat, Daisy, Laura and Jessie—equally, without our writing outings it would not have happened. I'm still sad none of you would purr on my lap.

To everyone at Janklow & Nesbit, both UK and US. Especially to Hellie, for holding my hand through every step and being a voice I can always trust, and to Kirby, for answering every neurotic email.

Last thanks always to Tom, the inspiration for a kind child who saw the world a little differently. Thank you for reading every word of this book aloud to me and doing all the voices. So excited for future adventures with you, my husband, and ever my best friend.